gs

"About that kiss."

"You don't have to apologize," Lauren said.

"I wasn't going to apologize," Shane said. "I enjoyed it. And I wouldn't mind repeating it sometime. But I didn't want it hanging between us, if it made you feel awkward or pressured or..."

"It was a good kiss. I'm just not interested in starting something when I'm not going to stick around. I'm here to find Courtney and Ashlyn, and then I'm going back to Denver."

"Denver isn't so far away."

"I know. But I have a bad habit of falling for men. Falling too hard, too soon. It's...awkward when things don't work out."

Was she saying she was falling for him? The idea made him a little light-headed. "It was a nice kiss. I'm not expecting more. You don't have to, either."

"But I think we should stick to looking for Courtney."

"All right." That was a reason for him to see her again. As for the rest—he might not have expectations, but he could hope.

DISAPPEARANCE AT DAKOTA RIDGE

CINDI MYERS

———

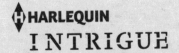

HARLEQUIN
INTRIGUE

For Jim and Loretta.

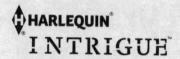

HARLEQUIN®
INTRIGUE™

ISBN-13: 978-1-335-48932-6

Disappearance at Dakota Ridge

Copyright © 2021 by Cynthia Myers

Recycling programs for this product may not exist in your area.

This edition published by arrangement with Harlequin Books S.A.

For questions and comments about the quality of this book, please contact us at CustomerService@Harlequin.com.

Harlequin Enterprises ULC
22 Adelaide St. West, 41st Floor
Toronto, Ontario M5H 4E3, Canada
www.Harlequin.com

Printed in U.S.A.

Cindi Myers is the author of more than fifty novels. When she's not plotting new romance plots, she enjoys skiing, gardening, cooking, crafting and daydreaming. A lover of small-town life, she lives with her husband and two spoiled dogs in the Colorado mountains.

Books by Cindi Myers

Harlequin Intrigue

Eagle Mountain: Search for Suspects

Disappearance at Dakota Ridge

The Ranger Brigade: Rocky Mountain Manhunt

Investigation in Black Canyon
Mountain of Evidence
Mountain Investigation
Presumed Deadly

Eagle Mountain Murder Mystery: Winter Storm Wedding

Ice Cold Killer
Snowbound Suspicion
Cold Conspiracy
Snowblind Justice

Eagle Mountain Murder Mystery

Saved by the Sheriff
Avalanche of Trouble
Deputy Defender
Danger on Dakota Ridge

Visit the Author Profile page at Harlequin.com.

CAST OF CHARACTERS

Lauren Baker—As a nurse practitioner, Lauren is used to looking after other people. When her brother's widow, Courtney, goes missing, Lauren must turn to the Eagle Mountain Sheriff's Department for help.

Deputy Shane Ellis—After an injury ended his career as a star baseball player, Shane returned to Eagle Mountain to start over as a sheriff's deputy. Helping Lauren Baker find Courtney would allow him to prove himself in his new career.

Courtney Baker—The young widow has lived a sheltered life and can be naive about other people, especially those who are interested in the fortune she inherited from her late husband.

Trey Allerton—The handsome veteran claims to have been Mike Baker's best friend. He persuades Courtney to help him build a ranch for troubled youth in the Colorado mountains, then both of them disappear.

Tom Chico—The older ex-con partners with Trey and Courtney to build their ranch, but his role in the venture is unclear.

Talia Larrivee—The rich young socialite is attracted to dangerous men, like Tom Chico.

Chapter One

Courtney would like it here, Lauren Baker thought as she drove through the town of Eagle Mountain, Colorado. A lover of beautiful old things, Courtney Baker would have felt at home among the gingerbread-trimmed Victorian buildings and carefully tended flower gardens. She would have marveled at the snowcapped mountains that soared above the town and would have been eager to explore the shops and cafés along the town's main street.

Lauren drove slowly, scanning the clusters of people on the sidewalks for the flash of Courtney's bright blond hair. But of course she didn't see anyone who looked like her sister-in-law. She had known before coming here that finding Courtney wouldn't be that easy.

The crisp female voice from her phone directed her to turn left ahead, and a few minutes later she pulled her Prius to the curb in front of the Rayford County sheriff's office. Stomach churning with nerves, she checked her appearance in the car's rearview mirror and smoothed a hand over her streaked brown hair, then slid out of the car and headed up the walk to the entrance to the sheriff's department.

A bell chimed as she entered the small lobby. "Hello," a woman said. "Can I help you?"

Lauren lowered her sunglasses and blinked at the white-haired woman behind the desk near the back of the lobby. The woman peered at Lauren from behind purple-framed eyeglasses and reached one pink-painted nail up to fondle a dangling earring shaped like a leaping dolphin. "Did you need something?" the woman prompted.

Lauren approached the desk. "I'd like to talk to someone about a missing person," she said.

The woman's eyebrows—carefully plucked and painted on—rose above the rim of her glasses. She picked up the phone at her right elbow. "Deputy Ellis," she said. "I'm sending a woman back to talk to you." She replaced the receiver and pointed toward a hallway to their left. "Go down that hall and take the first right. Deputy Ellis is the good-looking blond in the uniform."

Deputy Ellis—who was indeed good-looking, in a way that made Lauren catch her breath in spite of her distress—was waiting at the door of an office a little way down the hallway. "I'm Shane Ellis," he said, offering a firm, warm handshake and a steady gaze from tawny eyes. He was a big man—easily six foot four, with muscular legs and arms, thick blond hair swept over one brow and sculpted features. "Let's sit down and you can tell me how I can help you," he said, and ushered her into the office.

He indicated she should sit in one of the chairs in front of the battered desk, then instead of sitting behind the desk, he took the chair next to her. "What's your name?" he asked.

"Lauren Baker," she said.

"What brings you to Eagle Mountain? I don't think you're from around here. I have a good memory for faces, and I haven't seen yours before." In other circumstances, Lauren might have suspected this was a pickup line, but there was nothing flirtatious in his manner. Maybe he was trying to set her at ease.

"I'm from Denver," she said. "I came here to look for my sister-in-law, Courtney Baker. She's missing."

Deputy Ellis's brow furrowed. "Why don't you tell me your story," he said. "Start at the beginning." He leaned over to pluck a small recorder from the desk. "I'm going to record this, if you don't mind. It will help me keep things straight."

"Of course." She wanted him to remember everything she had to say. "Courtney is my brother's widow," she said. "They were married only two years before he was killed, in Afghanistan."

"I'm very sorry for your loss," the deputy said.

She nodded. "Courtney was devastated. We all were, but she was so young—only twenty-one at the time, and she was pregnant with Ashlyn. Courtney didn't have any family living near us, so I tried to help her. She and I became close." She focused on her knotted hands in her lap, trying to breathe past the pain of loss that had a habit of sneaking up on her at the most inconvenient times. Loss of her brother, and loss of a woman she had come to think of as her sister.

"When did Courtney go missing?" Ellis asked.

"First, I need to tell you that about three months ago a man named Trey Allerton came to see her. He said he had served with my brother, Mike, that they were best friends. He had some photographs of Courtney he said Mike had carried with him, pictures Trey said he felt duty bound to return to her. He said Mike had talked about her a lot and he had asked Trey to look after her if anything happened to him."

"You didn't like him much," Ellis said.

She jerked her head up and found his gold-brown eyes fixed on her. Sharp eyes, but not without compassion. "No, I didn't like him," she said. "I didn't believe his story about being Mike's best friend. I still have every letter and email and text Mike sent and he never mentioned Trey Allerton. And I didn't understand why Trey would have pictures of Courtney. The army had returned all of Mike's other personal belongings."

"What did Allerton want?" Ellis asked.

"He said he wanted to look after Courtney. If it had been me, I would have told him to get lost, but Courtney isn't like that. She—" How could she describe Courtney? *Needy* wasn't the right word, though it was partly true. *Weak* wasn't right, either. She had worked hard to pull her life together and to take care of her daughter after Mike died, showing a strength Lauren admired. "Courtney is very trusting. She always believes the best in everyone. She grew up in a small town, the only child of parents who protected her from everything. And then she met my brother and he protected her. Trey Allerton promised to protect her and I think that appealed to her."

"Protect her from what?"

"I don't know. Life, I guess." She sighed. "Anyway, he started hanging around, and within a week he was talking about his plan to buy a place in the mountains and build a ranch that could be a retreat center for disadvantaged kids. He painted a glowing picture—he even said he and Mike had planned to run the place together. Again—my brother never said anything about this to me or to anyone else that I could find. But Allerton made Courtney believe everything he said was true. The next think I knew, he had talked her into moving to Eagle Mountain with him to start this ranch."

Ellis jutted his chin, considering. He had an energy, a charisma that seemed out of place in a cop. But what did she know? She didn't have a lot of experience with law enforcement. "Did Allerton ask your sister-in-law to finance this supposed youth ranch?" he asked.

She felt a surge of elation. She had told him very little, but already Deputy Ellis had grasped the situation. "Oh, yes."

"How much money? Did he name a figure?"

"I don't know. But he must have known Courtney has money. A lot of it. My parents died right after Courtney and Mike married and before he left for Afghanistan, and Mike arranged for a trust that will provide his widow and his daughter a very good income for the rest of their lives. It's not the sort of thing Mike would have ever talked about, but somehow Allerton found out about it."

"All right. So your sister-in-law and Trey Allerton moved to Eagle Mountain? When was this?"

"Two weeks ago," she said. "I had a couple of texts

from Courtney, saying they had arrived in town and how much she loved it, and that they were going to talk to some people about buying land for the ranch. The last time I talked to her, shortly after they arrived here, she sounded off. She said she was fine and that I shouldn't worry, but the words didn't ring true—as if she was saying what Trey told her to say. Since then—nothing." She held up her hands. "She doesn't return my texts or phone calls, and there's nothing on her social media pages since then, either."

"And that's unusual?"

"Yes. Courtney posted multiple times a day to Facebook and Instagram, and she and I texted all the time." She leaned toward him, her gaze steady, trying to impress upon him the seriousness of the situation. "Something is wrong. I know it. I finally decided to come here to try to find out what's going on, but I need your help."

"Has anyone else heard from Courtney in the past week—other relatives or friends?"

"As far as I know, she wasn't close to any relatives. Her parents died shortly before she met Mike, and her grandparents have been gone for a while. She never mentioned any aunts and uncles or cousins she was in touch with."

"What about friends? Neighbors?"

Lauren shook her head. "No one has heard from her."

He studied her a long moment. She felt the intensity of his gaze, and forced herself to meet it with a level look of her own. "If you spoke to your sister-in-law and she said she was all right, that doesn't give us cause to go looking for her," he said finally.

"I know Courtney. I know she isn't all right." She leaned toward him. "Isn't there something called a welfare check? Can't you do that? Especially since there's a child involved?"

"Maybe." He leaned past her to slide a legal pad across the desk. "Let me get some details. Full name, description, things like that."

Lauren opened her purse and took out a five-by-seven studio portrait of Courtney, with two-year-old Ashlyn on her lap. "This was taken in May," she said.

Deputy Ellis studied the image of the young woman and the toddler, both with white-blond curls and large blue eyes. Ashlyn was laughing at something the photographer was doing, mouth open, eyes crinkled, hands in the act of clapping. Courtney's closed mouth curved slightly into a smile, but her eyes held the sadness that never really left her. For one so young, she had lost so much. Lauren was determined Trey Allerton didn't take even more. Lauren passed over an index card on which she'd written everything she knew about Courtney— approximate height and weight, cell phone number and social media handles. Lauren's contact information was underneath this. Ellis studied the list, then met her gaze again, his own questioning. "You know her Social Security number?"

"I helped her do her taxes last year and I still had a copy on my computer. I told you, we're close."

He nodded and placed the photograph and index card on the desk. "Do you have a photo of Trey Allerton?" he asked.

"Of course. I should have thought of that." She took

out her phone and scrolled through her saved pictures, until she came to one of Courtney with Trey. She turned the phone toward Deputy Ellis. "I took this last month." There was nothing sinister about the image of Courtney with the handsome, smiling man, but looking at it now made Lauren uneasy. How could she convey to the deputy just how much she distrusted Trey?

"Do you know where Courtney and Allerton were staying in Eagle Mountain?" he asked.

"She said they were at the Ranch Inn."

"Are you staying there now?"

"No. I'm in a vacation rental. I took a leave of absence from my job, and I intend to stay as long as it takes to find Courtney."

"What's your job?"

"I'm a nurse practitioner."

He stood, and she rose also. "What do you think has happened to your sister-in-law?" he asked.

She fought back the jumble of horrifying images that had crowded her sleepless nights and tried to maintain an appearance of calm. She wanted this man to take her seriously, not to think she'd been overdosing on crime dramas and imagining the worst. "I think Allerton may have persuaded her to cut contact with me, in an effort to swindle her out of her money. He's already taken advantage of her trust and innocence."

"I'll try to help," Ellis said. "But if your sister-in-law left of her own free will, there's not a lot we can do. There's no law against not talking to your relatives."

"No, but I can't abandon her. I need to make sure she's okay." She met his gaze again with a fierce look of her own. "Whatever Trey Allerton says, I'm the person Mike asked to look after Courtney and Ashlyn, and that's a promise I have to keep."

He nodded. "I'll be in touch."

She left the office feeling empty and restless. She had told Deputy Ellis everything she knew, but now she had to wait and trust that he was good enough at his job to find Courtney. He had struck her as sharp and competent.

She paused before getting into her car and looked up at the mountains that towered over the town. Courtney would love Eagle Mountain, but would Eagle Mountain love her?

"WHAT DID YOU say to her? She looked pretty upset when she left."

The door had scarcely closed behind Lauren Baker when Adelaide Kinkaid, office manager and Eagle Mountain's number one busybody, was at Shane's side, fixing him with a critical eye that always made him feel about ten years old. "Her sister-in-law has stopped talking to her," he said. "That's why she's upset. Not because of anything I said."

Adelaide pressed her bright pink lips together. Though she had to be pushing seventy, she dressed like someone fifty years younger, in bold colors and often downright garish accessories. But the look worked for her. "Did she know who you are? Is she a fan?"

"I'm a cop, Addie. That's all she cared about."

"Plenty of people still remember you," Adelaide said. "You can use that to your advantage."

Shane didn't see any advantage to being a *former* Major League pitcher, especially when it came to enforcing the law. When he did meet fans, they wanted to relive big games or, worse, talk about the injury that had sidelined him for good. They talked like his best years were over and he'd never do anything good again.

"Ms. Baker was worried about her sister-in-law," he said. "That's all that matters."

"She was very attractive," Adelaide said. "About your age."

Shane scowled. "I don't need you to find women for me, Addie," he said. He'd dated models and actresses when he was a pro ballplayer. Since coming back home to Eagle Mountain to settle down, he'd enjoyed working his way through the slate of eligible single women. If anything, they were even more fun than the models and actresses. He liked women in general, and he was in no hurry to settle down.

Adelaide made a huffing noise. "I would never try to saddle some poor woman with the likes of you."

Sure she wouldn't. They both turned at the sound of footsteps down the hall, to see Sheriff Travis Walker coming from the employee entrance. Almost as tall as Shane, Travis had a rangier build, and a famously reserved demeanor. Locals joked that when the sheriff gave a speech, the whole thing fit on a single note card. He stopped in front of Shane and Adelaide. "Something up?"

"A young woman came in to report a missing person," Adelaide said, before Shane could answer.

Travis looked at Shane, waiting.

Shane retrieved the photo from his desk and handed it to the sheriff. "Her name is Courtney Baker. She supposedly came to Eagle Mountain with a man named Trey Allerton, then dropped off the map. She stopped posting to social media and doesn't return phone calls or texts. Her sister-in-law, Lauren Baker, says that is really unlike Courtney and she's worried something has happened to her."

Travis studied the photograph. "Who's the kid?"

"Ashlyn Baker—Courtney's daughter. She's two, and is supposed to be with her mother."

"Where's the baby's father?" Adelaide leaned in to look at the picture.

"He died in Afghanistan over two years ago," Shane said. "Lauren Baker is his sister."

Travis returned the photograph to Shane. "How does Ms. Baker know they were in Eagle Mountain?" he asked.

"Her last communication with Courtney was about two weeks ago, phone call saying they were here and staying at the Ranch Inn," Shane said. "She also said she was fine and not to worry, but Ms. Baker insists something about the conversation wasn't right. She asked us to do a welfare check, though to do that, I need to find Courtney. I thought I'd start by asking at the motel."

Travis nodded.

"Have you heard of Trey Allerton?" Shane asked. He glanced from Travis to Adelaide, including them both in the question.

"No, but I'll ask around," Adelaide said. "There are a few women in this town who make a point of noticing every new young man who comes to town—and some not-so-young ones."

"Shane has got this," Travis said. He left them and went into his office.

"I guess if anyone at the motel saw these people, they'll tell you," Adelaide said. "You have a way of getting people to talk." The phone started ringing, and she left to answer it.

Shane stood outside his office, Courtney Baker's picture in hand. Unlike her happy baby, Courtney looked sad, and a little lost. Could a washed-up baseball player turned sheriff's deputy really help someone like her? After all, sometimes people took a deliberate wrong turn in life and all you could do was step back and wait for the crash.

Unless you were the Lauren Bakers of the world. People like Lauren didn't wait for a crash. They rushed to set up roadblocks, threw tacks on the road to puncture tires and, if all else failed, enlisted the nearest cop to issue a speeding ticket.

That was Shane, duly enlisted. He returned to his desk, tucked the photo and the file card into an envelope, and put on the wide-brimmed Stetson that completed his uniform. Time to get to work and see if he still had what it took to bring in a win.

Chapter Two

Lauren had chosen her vacation rental based on its central location in town and its reasonable price. She had reserved the apartment for a week and hoped her search wouldn't take longer. But she had a month's leave from her job and was willing to devote all of it, or more, to finding Courtney and making sure she was okay. Lauren owed that to Mike.

"You should have everything you need, but let me know if you run out of anything." Brenda Prentice, an attractive blonde, led Lauren up the outside stairs to the garage apartment next to her stylish home not far from the sheriff's department. "The cleaners come on Wednesdays. They'll take the trash out for pickup Thursday morning." She unlocked the door, then handed Lauren the key. "There's a map of the town and some brochures about local attractions if you're interested." She indicated a notebook on the table by the door.

"I'm sure I'll be very comfortable here." Lauren set down her bag and surveyed the clean, well-decorated apartment. It was a nice step up from a motel room, but she wasn't picky.

"What brings you to town?" Brenda asked.

Lauren's first instinct was to make a benign comment about taking a break or getting away, but if she was going to find Courtney, she needed to talk to as many people as possible. In a town as small as Eagle Mountain, anyone might have seen Courtney or know something about her. "I came here to look for my sister-in-law," she said. "We've lost touch, and the last I heard, she was here in Eagle Mountain."

Brenda had an expressive face, and her look of concern now seemed genuine. "Who is your sister-in-law?"

"Her name is Courtney Baker. She's traveling with her little girl, Ashlyn. Ashlyn is two." Lauren pulled up Courtney and Ashlyn's photo on her phone—the same one she had given Deputy Ellis. "This is them," she said. "It was taken just a couple of months ago."

Brenda studied the picture. "I'm sorry, I don't recognize her."

Lauren pushed aside her disappointment. She had known that finding Courtney might not be easy. "She may be traveling with a man named Trey Allerton." She showed Brenda Trey's photo. "Is he familiar?"

Brenda shook her head. "But I can ask my husband. He's a sheriff's deputy."

The words jolted her. But she reminded herself that Eagle Mountain was a small town. "I stopped by the sheriff's department on my way into town and spoke to a Deputy Ellis," she said.

Brenda smiled. "Oh, Shane." The words carried a lilt of amusement and maybe admiration.

"What do you mean, 'Oh, Shane'?" Lauren asked.

Brenda shook her head. "Nothing. He's a good deputy. He's also the local heartthrob." She grinned. "He caused quite a stir among the local women when he joined the force six months ago."

"He promised to try to find out more about Courtney and Trey Allerton," Lauren said. "But I got the impression that unless I could prove a crime had been committed, the bulk of the search was going to be up to me."

"Do you think a crime has been committed?" Brenda asked. "Did Allerton bring your sister-in-law here against her will?"

"I don't know." Lauren suppressed a sigh. "I just know that I haven't heard from Courtney at all in a week, and that's really not like her. And I don't trust Trey Allerton. I'm determined to stay in Eagle Mountain until I find them, or find out where they've gone."

"I have you down for a week here," Brenda said.

"Yes. I may need to stay longer."

Brenda shook her head. "I wish I could accommodate you, but this place is booked the rest of the summer. I can give you the name of a local real estate agent who might be able to help you with another rental. And I'll ask around and see if anyone I know has anything available."

"Thank you. Maybe I'll get lucky and I won't need it."

"I'll ask about your sister-in-law and Allerton, too," Brenda said. "It's hard for new people to come to a town this small without someone noticing them."

"I guess that's a good thing," Lauren said. "I didn't

realize before coming here that Eagle Mountain was quite so small."

"You sound as if something about that worries you," Brenda said.

The woman was definitely observant. "No offense to Deputy Ellis or your husband," Lauren said. "But does the sheriff's department in a town as small as Eagle Mountain have the resources to deal with this if it turns out to be a crime like kidnapping?"

"I think they probably are better equipped to handle a case like this than many larger departments," Brenda said. "Since we don't have much serious crime around here, the officers will have more time to devote to the search for your sister-in-law. Also, the officers tend to know everyone in the county. Someone new or anyone who is acting oddly will stand out. And the small-town stereotype of everyone knowing what everyone else is doing can be an advantage in any kind of investigation."

"I guess you have a point," Lauren said, though her doubts lingered.

"I'll leave you now, but my number is in that notebook." Brenda indicated the notebook on the table again. "Call me if you need anything at all or have any questions. And I'll let you know if I hear anything about your sister-in-law."

"Thanks."

When she was alone again, Lauren carried her bag into the bedroom, intending to unpack. But instead of opening the bag, she sat on the end of the bed and pulled out her phone. She pulled up Courtney's cell phone number and tried for the hundredth time to call. A mechanical voice informed her that the party she had called was unavailable and her voice mailbox was full.

She scrolled to her last texts from Courtney. Dinner with Trey tonight. He says he has big news about the ranch. I'll fill you in later.

Then, two days later, after numerous unanswered texts and calls from Lauren, she received a new message. Sorry. Super busy. We're going to see property for the ranch.

Allerton had painted a glowing picture of the ranch he and Mike had dreamed of opening—a place in the Colorado mountains where disadvantaged and troubled youth could come for fresh air, exercise, attention from caring adults and lessons in life skills. Courtney, who loved children and had a soft spot for anyone in need, had latched on to his appeal that this would be a way of securing her husband's legacy, and using his family money to do real good in the world.

Except that Mike had never once mentioned the idea of this ranch, to Courtney or to his sister. When Lauren had pointed this out, along with the fact that Allerton had no credentials that qualified him to run this kind of program, Courtney had dismissed her concerns. Mike probably hadn't wanted to tell her until he and Trey had worked out all the details, she had argued. And they could always hire professional counselors and therapists to work with the kids. The important thing was to find a place to build the facility and make the dream a reality.

Right. And all that took was money. Lots of it. Which Allerton didn't appear to have, but Courtney, thanks to Mike's generous trust, did.

Everything about Trey Allerton rubbed Lauren the wrong way. His smile was too broad, his words too glib, his charm too overdone. But Courtney saw none of that. He got to her by talking about Mike, sharing stories of their time in Afghanistan that Courtney was hungry to hear.

Courtney believed every word the man said, but Lauren wasn't that trusting. Maybe it came of her medical training and knowing how often people lied about the simplest things, from their weight to how many drinks they had a week, to the severity of their symptoms. Little of what Allerton said rang true to her. He obviously had known Mike. He knew plenty of personal details that convinced Courtney, but Lauren couldn't picture her brother being friends with someone like Allerton. Mike had disdained pretense and posturing. Growing up with wealth had given him a good eye for someone who was interested only in his money, something he and Lauren shared.

But Courtney trusted everyone. The only daughter of a minister who had spent most of her life in a small town in the Midwest, Courtney saw the good in everyone. She'd never encountered real evil, so she never looked for it in others. Mike loved that about her, but he also recognized she was vulnerable. "Look out for Courtney while I'm deployed," he had told Lauren. "Don't let anyone take advantage of her."

Lauren had solemnly promised to do so. But she had failed to keep her promise when it came to Trey Allerton.

She scrolled through the texts from that last week,

cryptic messages with Courtney pleading she was busy and couldn't talk. Don't worry. I'm fine. We're in a beautiful place called Eagle Mountain. And get this—the motel we're staying at is the Ranch Inn. I think that's a good sign, don't you?

What are you doing there? Lauren had replied.

Trey says I shouldn't talk about it yet. Don't worry. Everything will be fine.

Those last words sent a chill through Lauren. Everything was not fine, and the very fact that Courtney kept insisting it was made Lauren believe her sister-in-law knew she was in trouble, even if she wasn't ready to admit it.

"TAYLOR, YOU ARE just the person I needed to speak to." Shane leaned over the front desk of the Ranch Inn motel and grinned at the young woman behind it.

Taylor Redmond flushed pink. "Why would you want to talk to me, Shane?" she asked. "Do you think I'm guilty of something?"

"We're all guilty of something," he said.

She giggled. "I'm always glad to see you, Shane. What can I do for you?"

"I'm looking for a woman who stayed here recently. Name of Courtney Baker. She would have had a two-year-old girl with her, her daughter. And she might have been traveling with a man named Trey Allerton."

Twin lines formed between Taylor's eyebrows as she thought. "Those names don't sound familiar, but let me check our records." She moved to the computer terminal at the end of the counter and began typing. A few seconds later, she shook her head. "I'm not showing anyone registered under either of those names. Are you sure she was staying here?"

"This is her picture." He handed over the photo Lauren had given him. "Does she look familiar?"

Taylor's face brightened. "Oh, I remember her. Her little girl was so sweet. But she said her name was Allen. I never heard her first name. Just Mr. and Mrs. Allen. She and her husband and daughter stayed here earlier in the month." She turned to the computer once more and began typing. "They checked out eight days ago."

"What's his first name?"

"Troy. Troy Allen. Mister and missus. No first name for her. But I heard her call the little girl Ashley, I think."

"Ashlyn?"

"Maybe. Something like that. Why? Have they done something wrong?"

"Not that I know of." He slid the photograph back into its envelope. "Did everything seem okay with them? I mean, did the two of them get along and seem comfortable with each other?"

Taylor frowned again. "I guess so. I mean, they seemed normal to me, but I only saw them for a few minutes. What's going on? You can tell me."

"I'm just trying to get in touch with them. Did they say where they were headed next when they checked out?"

"I never talked to them. They just left the key in the

room on their last day. The bill was already paid, but a lot of people do that."

"Thanks, Taylor. You've been a big help."

She leaned across the counter toward him. "Before you go, I was wondering if you're planning on going to the Fireman's Ball July Fourth weekend."

"They're still doing that?" Shane had memories—some of them rather hazy—of attending the annual ball in the years before he was recruited to the majors.

"Oh, for sure." Taylor's eyes sparkled. "You know Eagle Mountain goes all out for the holiday. The town is packed with tourists. The ball kicks off everything."

"I wouldn't miss it," he said.

"Then maybe I'll see you there." She fluttered her eyelashes.

He took a step back. "Maybe you will," he said, and hastily retreated. Not that he didn't like Taylor, but she couldn't have been more than nineteen. Ten years younger than him, which wasn't so young, but a man in his position in a town this size had to be careful. So far, he'd stuck to women close to his age and older, never letting things get too serious. He wasn't ready to settle down yet, but he didn't want to get a reputation as a player who used women. He tried to remain friends with every woman he had ever dated and so far had succeeded.

Back in his cruiser, he made note of the information Taylor had given him about Courtney Baker and Trey Allerton. Apparently, Courtney hadn't behaved like a woman who was traveling with a man against her will. Lauren Baker might not approve of the man her brother's widow was associating with, but so far, Shane hadn't found evidence of a crime.

Except—why would a man who had nothing to hide check into a motel with an assumed name? Instead of focusing on Courtney Baker, maybe Shane should dig deeper into Trey Allerton's background.

Chapter Three

"This is a picture of my sister-in-law, Courtney, and her daughter, Ashlyn. They were in Eagle Mountain a couple of weeks ago. I was wondering if you remember seeing them in your store?" After visiting six stores along the town's main street Tuesday morning, Lauren had her spiel down pat. She passed the copy of Courtney and Ashlyn's photograph to the woman behind the counter of the toy store. The window display of a doll's tea party was the kind of thing that would have caught Courtney and Ashlyn's attention and might have enticed them in to browse, or even make a purchase.

The woman, a trim sixtysomething with fashionably cut short white hair, adjusted her silver-framed glasses and studied the photograph before handing it back to Courtney. "I'm sorry. I don't remember anyone like that. Such a cute little girl. And the woman is very pretty, too. I think I would have remembered if I had waited on them."

"Thank you for taking the time to look." Lauren tucked the photo back into her purse. She had received similar answers from the other five shops on this side of the street.

"Is something wrong?" the woman asked. "Why are you looking for them?"

"I believe they're missing," Lauren said. "I'm doing everything I can to try to find them."

"Have you contacted the sheriff's office?" the woman asked. "Maybe they can help you."

"The sheriff's department is looking, too," Lauren said.

"I hope you find them," the woman said, then turned away as a customer approached the counter.

Lauren left the store and studied the next one: a shop specializing in cigars and imported tobacco. Not the sort of thing to attract Courtney's attention, and as far as she knew, Allerton didn't smoke. Next in line was a café, the Cake Walk. A steady stream of people filed in, as it was almost lunchtime. Would one of them remember seeing Courtney and Ashlyn? And how upset would the owners of the café be with Lauren if she interrupted customers' meals to ask?

"I've never eaten anything here that wasn't good." A familiar voice sounded just behind her. She looked over her shoulder and saw Deputy Shane Ellis. He touched the brim of his Stetson in a gesture that was a little old-fashioned and completely charming. "I was just heading in for lunch," he said. "Would you join me?"

Her first instinct was to say no. She wasn't interested in socializing with this man, or with anyone, really. But lunch would give her a chance to find out what he had done so far to locate Courtney, and maybe to impress upon him that her sister-in-law wasn't behaving normally. Lauren believed Courtney really was in trouble, and she needed Deputy Ellis to believe it, too. "Thank you," she said, and forced a smile. "I'd love to."

He held the door open and touched her back lightly to usher her inside. Again, the gesture was mannerly, not intrusive. It made her feel cared for, a little vulnerable and a lot uncomfortable. She sat at an empty table and pulled up her chair before he could help her. He took the seat across from her, amusement in his eyes. "You can relax," he said. "I don't bite."

She wanted to deny that she was tense, but that was clearly a lie. "I'm not used to being in a situation like this," she said.

"Having lunch with a man?" He quirked one eyebrow. "Or with a cop?"

"I'm not used to being in an unfamiliar place, looking for a missing loved one," she said.

"Well hey, Shane!" The waitress, young and blonde, her hair in a ponytail, smiled at Ellis, ignoring Lauren entirely. "It's always good to see your handsome face in here."

"Hello, Dee," he said. "How's life treating you?"

"Well enough, though it could be better. What can I get for you?"

Shane looked at Lauren. "Do you need more time?" he asked.

Lauren turned to study the chalkboard that listed the day's special. "I'll have the soup and a house salad," she said.

"The green-chili burger for me," he said.

"Gotcha."

Dee moved away, and Shane turned to Lauren once more. "I heard you've been asking questions around town."

Had he been following her? Or had someone called the sheriff's office to report her? "I didn't come here to sit in my rental and wait for other people to do all the work," she said. "I thought if I could locate someone who had seen Courtney and Ashlyn, it would help me put together a time line of their movements."

"You're free to talk to anyone you want," he said. "Have you found anyone who remembers seeing your sister-in-law or her little girl?"

"No one remembers seeing them, and that in itself strikes me as wrong. Courtney loved to shop. And she especially loved cute little stores like the ones here in Eagle Mountain. She couldn't pass one by without stopping. Yet no one remembers her coming in to any of them."

"She and Allerton checked out of the Ranch Motel eight days ago," he said. "I don't think it's that unusual that people don't remember a customer they may have seen only a few minutes more than a week ago."

"Someone would have remembered Courtney," Lauren said. "You saw her picture. She's gorgeous. Striking. And Ashlyn is adorable. Someone would have remembered if they had been in one of those stores." The server returned with their drink orders.

"Thanks, Dee," Shane said, and was rewarded with a dazzling smile. Maybe he didn't see the disappointment in the server's eyes when he turned back to Lauren, but

Lauren did. Brenda Prentice hadn't been kidding when she said Shane was the local heartthrob.

"How do you know they checked out of the motel eight days ago?" she asked.

"I had the desk clerk check the registration records at the motel."

"I asked, and no one had heard of Courtney or Allerton," Lauren said.

"They weren't registered under their real names." He studied her over the rim of his glass, not saying more.

"How were they registered?" she prodded, annoyed that he was making her ask.

"You're not going to like the answer," he said.

"I don't like any of this, but I still want to know the truth."

"They were registered as Mr. and Mrs. Troy Allen."

She sucked in her breath. "This is worse than I thought, if he talked her into marrying him," she said.

"Do you think she would do that?" he asked.

"No!" She wanted to protest that Courtney was still too much in love with Mike to marry someone else, but her brother had been dead more than two years. Courtney had every right to fall in love and marry again. Just because the idea hurt to think of didn't mean it couldn't happen. "I don't think she was in love with Trey," she said. "She never talked about marrying him, but maybe that was because she knew I disapproved. And she may have thought he offered her and Ashlyn the kind of security and companionship she hadn't had since Mike died." She shook her head. "But I still can't believe it."

"Maybe they weren't married," he said. "People lie

about that kind of thing because they think it looks more respectable. Or because they don't want to attract attention or for a host of other reasons." He took a long sip of tea, then set down his glass. "For what it's worth, I didn't find any record of their marriage with the state of Colorado, though it sometimes takes a few weeks for the state to get the information from various counties. And if they were married in New Mexico or Nebraska, or another state, it wouldn't show up in a search of state records."

So he had been busy. "I'm impressed with what you've learned so far, Deputy Ellis," she said.

"Please, call me Shane," he said. "And is it okay if I call you Lauren?"

"Of course."

Dee returned and slid a steaming plate in front of him. "One green-chili burger for the hottest man in town," she said. She delivered Lauren's salad and soup without comment.

"Thanks." Shane picked up the burger. Dee lingered a moment, but when he said nothing else, she moved on.

He took a bite of burger and Lauren tried the soup. After a moment, Shane said, "I looked for a criminal record for Allerton, under both Allerton and Allen. I didn't find anything, but I've got some more feelers out."

"I had a friend check his military records," Lauren said. "He did serve in the same unit as Mike, and he was honorably discharged."

"You've saved me a step, then."

Loud laughter from across the room made them both

look over. A young woman with bright auburn curls, wearing an orange sundress with a print of blue-and-green parrots, swept into the café, trailed by two similarly striking women, all laden with shopping bags. They laughed loudly, catching the attention of everyone in the room. "Dee, show us your best table!" the redhead called, then joined the others in a new fit of giggles.

Dee scowled at them. "We only have one table, Talia," she said. "Take it or leave it."

"Well." Talia tilted her head, considering. "I suppose if we take it, that will automatically make it the best table."

More laughter as the trio followed a still-scowling Dee to the corner table. Lauren met Shane's gaze. "Who is that?" she asked.

"Talia Larrivee." He picked up his burger again. "I guess you could say she's the closest thing we have around here to a socialite."

More laughter erupted from the table as Dee arrived to take the women's order. "What makes her a socialite?" Lauren asked.

"She's Evan Larrivee's daughter."

"Evan Larrivee of Larrivee Software?"

"The same. He has a second home—or maybe a third or fourth home—just outside of town. I haven't been out there, but I hear it's quite the place."

"I'm sure you could charm her into showing you around the place if you really wanted to see it," Lauren said. "You seem to have most of the women in this town eating out of your hand."

"Not Ms. Larrivee." He popped a French fry into

his mouth, looking thoughtful. "I'm not rough around the edges enough for her. A little too much of a straight arrow."

"You seem to know a lot about her." Lauren tried to look unconcerned. Why should it matter to her what kind of relationship Shane had with the lovely Talia Larrivee?

"We've had a few encounters." He met her eyes. "Official ones."

"As in—she committed a crime?"

"Nothing major. And her father can afford the best lawyers to get his little girl out of trouble. But it's another reason she doesn't much care for me."

"How disappointing for you. She's very pretty. And rich."

"But not my type." His eyes met hers again, whiskey brown and mesmerizing.

Her heart beat a little faster and she found herself uttering the first thought that came to mind. "What is your type?"

"I like someone who's loyal. Someone who's competent and cool under pressure. Someone smart."

"I notice you don't mention beauty."

He shrugged. "Most women have something attractive about them. But yeah, I'm shallow enough to admit looks matter."

"Good luck finding this paragon," she said.

"Oh, I don't know. You seem to have a lot of those qualities." He pushed back his chair and stood. "I'll pay at the register," he said. "And I'll let you know if anything develops in the search for your sister-in-law."

He touched the brim of his hat again, then turned and sauntered away.

Lauren's weren't the only pair of female eyes on the deputy, but she was pretty sure she was the only one whose mouth was hanging open in shock.

Dee stopped by the table. "Can I get you anything else?" she asked. "More iced tea?"

Lauren pulled her gaze away from Shane's retreating back. "No, thank you."

"So, how do you know Shane?" she asked. "Is he an old friend?"

"No. My sister-in-law is missing and he's looking for her."

"Oh!" Dee's expression brightened. "So this was just a business lunch."

"Yes."

"Still, if you have to do business, why not with a guy like Shane?" Dee's attitude was friendly and confiding now. "He puts most other guys in this town to shame, but he's not full of himself, like you might expect." She began gathering up the empty plates and cutlery. "I couldn't believe my ears when I heard he was coming back to town. He could have gone anywhere—why here? And to be a deputy, of all things." She shook her head.

"Why are you surprised he's a deputy?" Lauren leaned back to allow Dee to retrieve her empty glass.

"I would have expected him to get work as a broadcaster, or maybe a coach." Dee added the glass to the bus tub and balanced the tub on one cocked hip. "I mean, isn't that what ballplayers do when they retire?"

"Wait a minute, he was a ballplayer? Basketball?"

"You didn't know? He was a pitcher. For the Colorado Rockies. A good one, too, until he tore up his arm." She shook her head. "Such a shame. You think he looks good in that deputy's uniform—you should have seen him in pinstripes. You sure you don't need anything else?"

"No, thank you." Lauren stood.

She made her way across the crowded café, aware of a few eyes watching her, though most were focused on Talia and her two friends as Talia loudly regaled them with a story about a drunken attempt at skinny-dipping in a nearby swimming hole. "The water was ice-cold!" she shrieked.

Lauren told herself she should show Courtney and Ashlyn's photo to the rest of the stores on Main, but she had lost the heart for it. Instead, she made her way back to the rental and booted up her laptop.

A search on the name Shane Ellis filled her screen with articles about the Colorado Rockies' ace pitcher, including dozens of pictures—mostly of Shane in uniform, but a few of him at parties or charity events, often with an attractive woman on his arm. The man she was familiar with looked a little older, a little less...*glamorous*, the best word she could think of. She had met Shane the small-town deputy. These pictures were of Shane the celebrity. The star athlete.

She opened the top article in the search and read about his retirement from professional baseball. It included an overview of his career: top pick while he was still in college, meteoric rise through the minor leagues, nomination for a Cy Young Award as a rookie pitcher, helped lead his team to the playoffs his second year, culminating with a career-ending injury. Surgery. A comeback attempt. Then the announcement that he was leaving baseball.

She sat back, trying to digest everything she had just read. She had to agree with Dee—it seemed odd that Shane had decided to become a small-town law enforcement officer. He had known fame and wealth, he was good-looking and charming, and he probably could have done anything he wanted with his life. Instead he had retreated to this out-of-the-way place. Why? How did prowess as a pitcher translate to crime solving?

Chapter Four

After lunch, Shane slipped through the back door of the sheriff's office and headed for his desk, hoping to catch up on some paperwork before Adelaide realized he was there. The office manager had a habit of sending members of the public to him first. "You're so good with people," she said when he had protested.

But Adelaide had ears like a cat's and he had scarcely sat down before she hurried to his side. "There's going to be a sheriff's department versus fire department baseball game on the Fourth to raise money to spruce up the Little League fields," she said.

Inwardly, he cringed, though he kept his expression neutral. "I hadn't heard," he said.

He pretended to read through the report on his screen, though the words were a blur.

"Better get your pitching arm warmed up," Adelaide said.

"Doesn't the department have a regular team? Maybe they won't want me."

Adelaide's laughter was more of a hoot. "Of course

they'll want you. And they'll need you to win. The fire department has some real sluggers on their team."

Tension settled between his shoulders. "I'm not a Major League pitcher anymore," he reminded her.

"You're miles better than anyone else around here."

"Better at what?" Sergeant Gage Walker strolled into the space devoted to the deputies' desks, which was generally known as the bullpen. The irony of going from one bullpen to another wasn't lost on Shane. Gage's brother, Sheriff Travis Walker, followed him into the room. Taller, blonder and definitely more outgoing than his brother, Gage had a sharp sense of humor and a quick mind.

"I was just telling Shane about the annual sheriff's department versus fire department ball game for the Fourth of July," Adelaide said.

"Those smoke eaters won't know what to do when they see the heat you bring," Gage said.

"It's been a while since I've pitched," Shane said.

Gage clapped a hand on his shoulder. "Then you'd better start practicing."

The front door buzzer sounded. "I'd better go see who that is," Adelaide said.

"I'll go with you," Gage said and followed her out of the room.

"Are you okay with pitching in the game?" Travis asked. "Does the arm still bother you?"

"Not really." Most of the time his arm felt fine. "But I don't have the speed and power I used to."

"This isn't the majors," Travis said. "The fire department has a few pretty good hitters, but anything you throw is going to get past them."

The sheriff's interest in the game surprised Shane. Travis was always so focused on his work first and his family second. He rarely engaged in debates about sports, though Shane had heard he'd been a pretty good athlete in high school. "What's at stake here?" Shane asked.

"Bragging rights, mostly. But the fire department has beat us the past four years running. It would be nice to take the title back."

"I'll do what I can," Shane said.

"You're liable to draw a crowd when word gets out you'll be on the mound," Travis said. "Does that bother you?"

Some. Only because people would expect to see the ace he'd been, not the above-average amateur he was now. "Nah, it's okay," he lied.

"Anything new on the missing woman?" The sheriff was all business again.

Shane filled him in on the information he'd gleaned from computer searches and the motel, and what he'd learned from Lauren at lunch. "The sister-in-law thinks Trey Allerton was after Courtney Baker's money. She's positive something shady is going on."

"See if you can find out what that is," Travis said. "But don't neglect more pressing business. This may be a case of a woman who wanted to get away from her late husband's family and start over. It happens."

"I'll keep that in mind."

Alone once more, Shane tried to focus on the motor

vehicle accident report he needed to complete, but his mind kept going back to the grief in Lauren's eyes when she spoke of her dead brother and his missing wife. Lauren didn't come across to him as a controlling relative. She was reserved and serious, but loyal and caring, too. She probably thought he was out of line, telling her she was the type of woman who interested him, but he'd hoped the confession—all truth—would shake her enough to get her to loosen up and trust him more. They were on the same side, both wanting to find her sister-in-law and niece safe and happy, but he could tell Lauren didn't believe he'd do a good job.

Others probably shared her doubts. He wasn't blind to the fact that everyone still saw him as a ballplayer first and a law enforcement officer second. He'd been a good player, gifted even—you had to be to make it to the majors.

Did he have the talent it took to be a good officer? Could he find Courtney Baker? He wouldn't mind seeing Lauren look at him the way female fans had sometimes regarded him when he wore a baseball uniform.

"Week-to-week rentals can be hard to come by in the summer. That's our busy season. But I might have a couple of places that would suit you," Mallory Workman said when Lauren stopped by Workman Realty on Wednesday. Mallory had the weathered skin of someone who spent a lot of time outdoors. She wore a pearl-button Western shirt, pressed slim jeans and pink cowboy boots, and a gold rodeo buckle Lauren suspected was the real deal. "I was state barrel racing champion in ninety-six," she said when she noticed Lauren taking in the buckle. "It's been a while, but I still ride, and I help train girls who are just starting out."

"I appreciate your help finding a place for me to stay after my week at Brenda Prentice's place runs out," Lauren said.

"Brenda is a real sweetheart," Mallory said. She sat at her desk and pulled up a form on her computer. "Let me get a little information from you and we'll go from there. I know you said week to week, but about how long do you think you'll need the place?"

"I wish I knew," Lauren said. "It really depends on whether or not I can make contact with my sister-in-law."

"You got a picture?" Mallory asked. "I know pretty much everyone in town, and between my job and the rodeo, I meet a lot of people who come through here."

Lauren handed over the photograph of Courtney and Ashlyn. Mallory studied it a long moment. "She's got the kind of looks that would make most people do a double take," she said after a moment. "And that little girl is a real doll."

"Here's a photo of the man they're supposed to be with," Lauren said, showing Trey's picture. "He's about six feet tall, and he can be very charming."

"And I'm guessing not a nice guy, from your tone of voice," Mallory said.

"I don't know him well," she admitted. "But it worries me that Courtney came here with him, and then cut off all communication. I haven't heard from her, and neither has anyone else who knows her."

"I haven't seen either of them around," Mallory said. "But I'll keep my ears open and let you know if I hear anything. What were they doing in Eagle Mountain?"

"Trey Allerton, the man Courtney is allegedly with, said he was looking for land in the mountains to open a ranch for disadvantaged youth. Kind of a summer camp setup, I guess."

"I haven't had anyone contact me about anything like that, but I'll ask around. All the agents here in town are friendly, and even though we're competitors, we share information and help each other out."

"Thanks. I'd really appreciate it."

"Now, let's get your information."

They had almost finished completing the form when the door to the office opened and Shane Ellis strolled in. "Hello, ladies," he said, touching the brim of his hat. His gaze fixed on Lauren. "We seem to keep running into each other."

"Lauren was just telling me about her missing sister-in-law," Mallory said. "I'm going to talk to some other agents in town and see if any of them got a call from this Trey Allerton."

"You're one step ahead of me," Shane said. "I was stopping by to ask if you'd met Allerton on his quest for his kids' ranch."

"You know where else you might check?" Mallory said. "You should look up recent sales at the courthouse. Maybe he already bought something."

"Would there have been time for that?" Lauren asked.

"You'd be surprised how quickly deals can close sometimes, especially if the buyer has cash."

"I don't think Allerton had that kind of money," Lauren said.

"What about Courtney?" Shane asked.

Lauren sucked in her lower lip, thinking. "I don't think so. The terms of her trust limit what she can withdraw cash for, but maybe I can do some checking."

"You do that, and I'll check at the courthouse," Shane said. "Mallory, you'll let us know if you hear anything from your competition?"

"Of course." Mallory's smile warmed. "And if I do you this favor, you'll owe me one."

He sat up straighter. "What's that?"

"One dance at the Fireman's Ball," Mallory said. "You are going, aren't you?"

"Wouldn't miss it."

Mallory turned to Lauren. "If you're here for the Fourth of July, you should plan to go to the dance. And there's a parade, and fireworks. Oh, and a baseball game." She grinned at Shane. "The annual rivalry between the sheriff's department and the fire department. That should be very interesting this year. I assume you're pitching for the sheriff's team?"

Shane shifted from foot to foot. "I guess so."

"I went to a Rockies game when Shane was pitching once," Mallory told Lauren. "It was thrilling. The team won, too. Made me feel proud to see a hometown boy doing so well."

"Yeah, well, I'd better get over to the courthouse before they close for lunch," Shane said.

Lauren stood. "I'll go with you."

Neither of them said anything until they were on the sidewalk. "You don't like talking about your baseball career, do you?" she said.

He shrugged. "I'm not one to live in the past."

The Rayford County Courthouse was an elegant structure made of large blocks of red native stone, three stories tall with a gray slate roof and galleries of long windows. Inside, their steps echoed on scarred hardwood floors. They passed through a metal detector and a guard inspected Lauren's purse, then Shane led her down a long hall to a door marked County Clerk.

"Hello, Frieda," Shane greeted the plump woman behind the counter, her blond hair in braids that reached almost to her waist, her lips slicked with bright pink gloss.

"Well, Shane Ellis, you handsome thing." Her voice was a honeyed Southern drawl. "What can I do for you?"

"This is Lauren Baker," Shane introduced her. "Lauren, Frieda Patterson, our county clerk. Frieda knows everyone and everything in the county."

"Everyone ends up in this office at one time or another," Frieda said. "If they buy property or get tags for their car or get a new RV, they've got to see me, so yes, I know everyone." She narrowed her eyes. "So who are you looking for?"

"A man named Trey Allerton," Shane said. "He came to town about three weeks ago to look for property to start a youth ranch. Do you remember any transactions like that?"

Frieda shaped her bright lips into a pout. "I haven't recorded any sales of big property or ranch land in the past month," she said. "What did this guy look like?"

Shane looked to Lauren. "Trey is about six feet, slim, with sandy hair and brown eyes," she said. "He can be very charming. He might have had this woman with him." She showed the photo of Courtney and Trey on her phone.

Frieda considered the photograph and shook her head. "I haven't seen them," she said, and returned the phone to Lauren. "But the man sounds familiar. But it wasn't a sale—it was a lease."

"Tell us about that," Shane said.

Frieda shook her head. "Not without permission from the landlord."

"Could you ask the landlord for permission to share that information with local law enforcement? Or give me their name and I'll contact them myself."

"I don't know how that would go over," she said. "Let me call them and see. I'll get back to you."

"Could you do it now?" He gave her his most charming smile.

"All right." She returned the smile. "Give me a minute."

She retreated to a back room and returned a few moments later. "Mr. Russell is always happy to cooperate with the sheriff's office," she said.

She moved to a computer terminal and began typing. "The man you're looking for wasn't using the name Allerton," she said after a moment. "He called himself Allen. Troy Allen."

"That's the name he used when he registered at the motel," Shane said.

"You should have said," Frieda chided. "I'd have remembered him sooner." She typed some more, and a printer behind her whirred. She collected the printout and laid it on the counter.

Lauren and Shane leaned over to read it. "This description of metes and bounds doesn't mean much to me," Shane said. "Can you translate it into plain English?"

"It's a section of the Russell Ranch," Frieda said. "Samuel Russell agreed to lease sixty acres to Allen Entertainment, Inc., for five years. They came in together to do the deal and Sam didn't look upset about it or anything."

"Thanks, Frieda."

"Anytime, darling." She slid the paper toward him. "I'm looking forward to seeing you pitch on the Fourth," she said. "I never got to see one of your games in person, but I watched you on TV."

"This won't be that exciting," he said.

"It will be for us," she said. "You're the closest thing we have to a celebrity."

He managed a pained smile, then he and Lauren left the courthouse. "I'll check out this property and let you know what I find," he said when they were outside again.

"I have a better idea," she said. "Take me with you."

"I can't take a civilian on sheriff's business."

"Civilians do ride-alongs with law enforcement officers all the time," she said. "Besides, so far we're following each other around town, covering the same ground. Wouldn't it be easier if we worked together?"

"When you say it like that, it makes perfect sense."

"I'm a very sensible person."

"Yeah. I like that about you." His eyes met hers and she felt a tug inside, like a guitar string snapping. Something letting go that she didn't understand—but didn't exactly want to run away from.

Chapter Five

The Russell Ranch sprawled across six hundred acres of sagebrush and pinion foothills and grassy valleys shadowed by towering mountain peaks. Shane eased the sheriff's department SUV down the rutted gravel road that led to the main entrance to the ranch. Lauren, beside him in the passenger seat, looked up at the massive iron gate with the Double R brand at its center. "Who owns the ranch?" she asked. "And why would they lease part of it to Trey Allerton?"

"Samuel Russell owns the place," Shane said. "He's third or fourth generation to ranch here. He had a son, Brock, but he was killed in an accident right after I graduated high school. He has a daughter, Willow, who was a few years behind me in school."

"Is there a Mrs. Russell?" Lauren asked.

"She died when the kids were pretty little. Sam never remarried, that I've heard, anyway. As for why he would lease the land, I intend to ask him."

He lowered the driver's window and pressed the call button on the intercom by the driveway.

"Hello?" a man's gruff voice demanded.

"Mr. Russell? This is Deputy Ellis. We spoke on the phone earlier."

"Gate's open. Come on up." As he spoke, the gate swung to the side. Shane raised the window and drove through. He drove another quarter mile before the ranch house came into view—red brick with green gables and shutters and a sharply pitched slate roof. He parked the SUV in the drive and a man walked out to meet them.

Samuel Russell had thick white hair, a deep tan, the bowed gait of a man who had spent a life on horseback and the deeply wrinkled face of someone who lived outdoors in all seasons. He shook hands with Shane and nodded to Lauren. "You said on the phone you wanted to talk to me about Trey Allerton, but there's not a whole lot I can tell you," he said.

"Anything you have to say might help us," Shane said. He squinted into the bright sun. "Is there someplace inside we can talk?" he asked.

"Sure."

Russell led the way up the steps and into a large entry tiled with red-brown Saltillo tile. He walked down a short, carpeted hallway and opened the door to an office, with a desk, computer and printer, and a pair of worn upholstered armchairs. Russell sank into one of the chairs. "This is where I met Allen when he came to talk to me about leasing that section of land. That's how he introduced himself—Troy Allen, though the name on all the paperwork was Trey Allerton."

"That didn't strike you as odd?" Shane asked.

"Sure. But people do a lot of odd things. My brother's name is Robert, but no one ever calls him that. Even his checks say Shorty Russell on them. This Allerton fellow's business was Allen Entertainment. My lawyer looked everything over and says the agreement is all aboveboard, so I don't guess I care what a man chooses to call himself."

Lauren sat in the chair across from him and Shane leaned against the desk. "How did he find out about the land?" Shane asked. "How did he know it was available?"

"I'd told a few people I'd be open to the right offer," Russell said. "Nothing formal, but word gets passed around. He probably heard about it from one of the real estate agents in town. They're always on the lookout for another deal. But he could have just as easily heard it down at the local bar, somebody running their mouth."

"But he contacted you, you didn't contact him, is that right?" Shane asked.

"That's right. He called me up and said he was looking for a place to start a ranch to host disadvantaged kids. A summer camp, or something. I told him the land wasn't much good for actual ranching, but it would probably be fine for that. So we arranged for him and his business partner to come see it."

"His business partner?" Lauren leaned toward him. "Who was that?"

"He never addressed him by name in my hearing," Russell said. "He was a little older than Allen, short and stocky, with dark hair. Rough looking."

"How do you mean?" Shane asked.

"He wore a long-sleeved shirt, but the cuff slipped up and I could make out tattoos down to his wrist. I'm no expert, but they looked homemade to me, like the kind men give each other in prison." He met Shane's gaze. "I've hired a few ex-cons to work for me before. I believe in giving a man a second chance. Sometimes it works out, sometimes it doesn't."

"Did Allen have a woman with him?" Lauren asked. "A young blonde woman, and a little girl?"

She offered the photo of Courtney and Ashlyn, and Russell nodded. "The woman was with him. Hard to miss her. No little girl, though. But there was another woman, about her age, but taller, with long red hair and a kind of restless manner. She was hanging on the tattooed guy pretty good and was acting—I don't know— off. Like maybe she was on something."

"You think she was on drugs?" Shane asked.

"I don't know. She was just—fidgety, and kind of spacey."

"Do you know the women's names?" Shane asked.

"Sorry, I don't."

"What happened when the four of them came to see you?" Shane asked.

"I drove them out to look at the place. Mr. Allerton did all the talking. He said he liked the place and offered me cash—ten thousand down and another ten thousand in two weeks."

"Why not the whole twenty thousand up front?" Shane asked.

"He said he was waiting on a check for some work he'd done."

"And you agreed?" Lauren said.

"I didn't see any reason not to," Russell said. "The

land is still mine, and if he violated the terms of the lease, I could kick him out."

"Did he pay you everything he owed?" Shane asked.

"He paid the first ten thousand," Russell said. "The rest isn't due for another week." He narrowed his eyes. "Are you trying to tell me I shouldn't hold my breath for that money?"

"Did Allerton tell you what his plans were for the property?" Shane asked. "Did he intend to live there?"

"He said he might move an RV onto the place to live in, and he wanted to build some cabins for the kids and other workers to stay in. I reminded him any buildings stayed with the property, and he agreed to that— didn't even blink. Which I thought didn't make him the shrewdest businessman in the world, but what did I care about that? I figured, in the end, I could wind up with a nice bunch of cabins on the land. Maybe I could turn it into a guest ranch or something."

"You didn't think Allerton's youth ranch was going to pan out?" Shane asked.

"Maybe it would, maybe it wouldn't. He was a good talker, but I thought he might be full of hot air. But like I said, I didn't see that I had a lot to lose."

"Did either of the women say anything?" Lauren asked.

Russell shook his head. "Not a peep. And nothing from the other man, either. Allen talked enough for all three of them."

"How many times did you meet with him?" Shane asked.

"Twice—that first time he came to see the place, and

again when we closed the deal. He came alone that time, with a cashier's check for the first payment. He didn't run his mouth as much that time, just did the paperwork, handed over the check and thanked me. A couple of other times after that I saw vehicles—a truck and a blue sedan—headed back toward the property he leased."

"When was the last time you saw them?" Shane asked.

Russell rubbed his chin. "I guess it's been a week or so, maybe a little less." He shrugged. "He and his friends didn't make any trouble, so I didn't have any reason to keep track."

"I'd like to see the property he leased," Shane said. "Then I may have more questions for you."

Russell stood. "You're welcome to drive back there. Just continue on this road past my gate, up a hill and around a big curve. You'll cross a cattle guard and that's the western boundary. There's an old trailer house back there, but it's not really fit to live in. I told Allen if he wanted to get rid of it, he'd have to pay to have it hauled away. He didn't have a problem with that."

"Thank you, Mr. Russell." Shane handed the rancher one of his business cards. "Let me know if you hear from Mr. Allen, or if you think of anything else."

"What's he done, that you're so interested in him?" Russell asked.

"The woman he's with is my sister-in-law," Lauren said. "She's my brother's widow, and I haven't heard anything from her for over a week. I want to make sure she's all right."

"She looked fine when I saw her," Russell said. "If that's any comfort to you."

Shane put a hand to Lauren's back and urged her toward the door. "Do the other people Russell described—the man and the woman who were with Trey—sound like anyone you know?" Shane asked when they were in the cruiser again.

"No," she said. "Mike never brought any other friends over when he and Courtney visited my place, and I never saw anyone else when I was with them at Courtney's house. I don't remember her mentioning anyone else, either."

She sat back, arms folded over her chest. "I can't believe Russell would lease his property to someone he hardly knew."

"He thought it was a way to get money from a section of the property he's not utilizing right now," Shane said. "And maybe Allerton impressed him with his plans to use the place to help kids."

"I don't believe Allerton has any intention of helping children," Lauren said. "I think he just said that to get to Courtney. Everything about the man struck me as phony, but she refused to see it." She crossed her arms over her chest and stared straight ahead.

"What did she say when you told her your opinion of Allerton?" Shane asked.

"She said I was upset because Trey survived and Mike didn't, and that I didn't want her to be with any man but Mike."

He winced. "Any chance she was on to something?"

She sat up straighter, and he could almost feel the

chill from the cold look she sent him. "This didn't have anything to do with Mike. I'm a good judge of character, and I recognize a snake when I see one."

"So if Courtney had decided to leave with a different man—someone you like—you wouldn't be here now looking for her," he said.

"If she ran off with this man and then stopped all communication with me and with all of her other friends, yes, of course I'd be concerned and I'd be searching for her. The fact that I don't like Allerton makes me even more afraid for her."

"Just making sure," he said. "I believe you, but I need to be able to justify devoting my time to driving out here with you. We haven't established a crime has been committed."

"Maybe we'll get some answers at the ranch," she said.

They both fell silent, gravel popping beneath the tires the only sound. This part of the ranch looked more used up than the other land, thick stands of silvery sagebrush and clumps of prickly pear cactus choking out the grass, signs of overgrazing. Shane rolled down the driver's window a few inches, bringing in the smell of sage and the raucous fussing of a flock of pinion jays.

Lauren pulled out her phone. "No service," she said.

"Maybe that's why you haven't heard from Courtney," he said.

"Surely she has to leave the ranch sometime," Lauren said. "Staying out here with just Ashlyn and Allerton for company would drive her crazy. Courtney isn't really a country girl. She likes her fancy coffee and professional manicures and getting her hair done once a month."

She made a good case for something to be wrong, but was that merely because she couldn't accept that her brother's widow had moved on? If they found Courtney and Ashlyn happily ensconced in a cozy cabin, getting the property ready to welcome a bunch of disadvantaged children, would Lauren be able to accept that, and move on herself?

The SUV rumbled across a cattle guard, and the silvery branches of a dead pinion marked the turn onto the twin ruts of a drive that twisted through a stand of sagebrush, then ended abruptly at a leaning trailer house. The trailer's siding, faded turquoise streaked with rust, bore several large dents, as if a truck or other vehicle had collided with it. The screen door—minus all but a remnant of screen—stood open, and the windows, dirty and uncurtained, looked onto a rocky clearing.

"Stay here while I check this out," Shane said.

But as soon as he was away from the SUV, Lauren came after him. "Courtney doesn't know you," she said. "She might not answer the door."

He had a feeling no one was going to answer the door here. The trailer didn't look as if anyone had lived in it for the last decade. He climbed the three wooden steps to the door, his boots making a hollow echo with each footfall. He knocked firmly, then waited. Lauren stood on the step just below him, her shoulder brushing his arm. "I don't hear anything," she whispered.

He knocked again, and when no answer came, he

tried the doorknob. It turned easily in his hand and swung open with a creak worthy of a nightmare.

The carpet in the living room had once been avocado green, the color discernable now only in bright patches where furniture had once stood. The only items in the room now were a broken plastic patio chair and an overturned cardboard box that had once held paper towels. "Hello!" Shane called. "Anybody home?"

Absolute silence met his inquiry. He moved forward, one hand hovering near his gun, constantly scanning the empty room for any sign of movement. They checked the kitchen, to the left of the living room, a rust-streaked sink and yellow laminate countertops identifying its function. Beyond that was a bedroom, with no bed, only a stack of newspapers. The top one was dated five years previous. "I don't think anyone has been here in a long time," he said, dropping the paper onto the pile once more.

Lauren moved past him, into the bathroom, with its plastic tub and shower combo and toilet. "Nothing but dirt in here," he said.

"Wait a minute." She bent and retrieved something from the tub.

Shane stared at a doll, about six inches high with long purple hair. The doll wore a pink dress with a yellow daisy embroidered in one corner. Lauren's hand holding the toy trembled, and when he met her gaze, he was shocked to see her eyes filled with tears. "Ashlyn was here," she said. "This is hers. Why would she have left it behind?"

Shane acted on instinct, not as a cop, but as a man

who hated to see another person in distress. He put an arm around her shoulder. "It's good to know she was here," he said. "It means we're on the right track. And children forget things. They get distracted. Finding it here doesn't mean anything bad happened."

She nodded, her eyes still fixed on the doll. "You're right." She took a deep breath. "They were here. So where did they go?" She looked into his eyes, tears gone, the determination he had admired so much returned. "And how are we going to find them?"

Chapter Six

Lauren stared at the little doll, a clear picture in her mind of Ashlyn playing with it. She had fallen in love with the purple-haired toy and carried it everywhere. "Ashlyn isn't careless," she said. "She wouldn't just leave her doll behind."

"Maybe something else distracted her and she laid the doll down, thinking she'd come back to her," Shane said.

"So why didn't she come back?" Her imagination could think of a dozen different reasons Ashlyn and Courtney would have failed to retrieve the doll, none of them good.

"I don't know," he said.

She smoothed the doll's hair, then offered it to him. "I guess you'll want this," she said.

He didn't take the doll. "You should keep it."

"But don't you want to log it in as evidence?"

He frowned. "Evidence of what?"

"It proves Ashlyn was here," she said. "And if she was here, Courtney must have been here."

"Yes, it could be proof that they were here," he said.

"But Mr. Russell already told us Allerton came here. He had a legitimate lease, so him being here isn't a crime." He looked around the empty trailer. "There's no sign of a struggle, or of anything illegal here. I don't have any reason to treat this as a crime scene."

She wanted to argue with him, to protest the facts that Ashlyn and Courtney weren't here now and that Ashlyn had left behind her beloved doll were proof that something was wrong. But that was only her instinct. She had no real evidence that this was so. "What are you going to do?" she asked.

"I'm going to try to learn more about the man and the woman who were with Allerton and Courtney when they visited Mr. Russell."

Relief surged through her. "Then you're not going to give up."

"I'm not going to give up," he said. "But this can't be my only focus."

"I understand." She didn't want to. The fate of her sister-in-law and her niece felt so important to her. But she had a job that placed many demands on her, too. It would have been irresponsible for her to devote all her energy to one patient when so many other people needed care. It was the same with law enforcement. "I'm grateful for anything you can do," she said.

"Are you ready to go?" he asked.

She nodded.

They left the trailer and made the drive back to town in silence. Lauren stared out the window of the SUV, taking in the beautiful but wild scenery—vast stretches of wooded mountainsides or open valleys carpeted with wildflowers, with no houses or other people in sight. What if Courtney and Ashlyn were lost somewhere out in that wilderness? Or what if they were trapped with Allerton and the mysterious couple Mr. Russell had mentioned, desperate to get away but unable to do so?

"I'm sorry I can't do more to help." Shane interrupted her thoughts as they neared the sheriff's department. "Television and movies make it seem like a department can throw everything they've got at a single case, especially a missing person. But we can't really do that in real life." He spoke gently, as if he didn't want to upset her any more than she already was.

She turned toward him and managed a faint smile. "I know," she said. "I don't like it much, but I understand. I'm going to keep doing everything I can on my part to find them, too."

He parked in front of the sheriff's department and shut off the engine, but when she started to open the door, he put a hand on her arm. "Don't do anything reckless," he said. "If you find out something you think is important, tell me about it. Don't go rushing into a situation that might be trouble."

"I won't, but—"

"No buts," he said. "I know I said I couldn't make this a priority, but I don't want you thinking you should act on your own because you don't want to bother me or because you think I won't pay attention. I will pay attention. To you."

His hand on her arm was warm and firm, almost a caress. She heard the care in his voice and saw it in his eyes, and her heart fluttered, unsettling her. "Thank you," she said, and opened the door.

He took his hand away. "I'll touch base with you soon," he said.

She nodded. "Thanks." She'd look forward to talking to him again. And not just because of the case. There was something special about this man who was so considerate of her feelings, and so earnest in his desire to help. He didn't fit her image of a famous athlete or a small-town cop.

She returned to the rental apartment, intending to start calling the list of potential rentals Mallory Workman had emailed to her. Instead, she found herself replaying their conversation with Samuel Russell. He'd said that Troy Allen / Trey Allerton had paid him the first lease payment and promised another $10,000 in two weeks. Nothing about Allerton had indicated to her that he had much money. He drove an older-model pickup truck that was well cared for but not expensive. He dressed well but not extravagantly. And he never talked about having money. That didn't mean he didn't have substantial savings or an inheritance, but he had always stressed the need for Courtney to "invest" in the ranch with him, telling her this was what Mike would have wanted.

She took out her phone and punched in a number. "Addison, Simmons and Clark," a woman's crisp voice answered.

"Mindy? It's Lauren Baker."

"Lauren! It's always nice to hear from you. How have you been?" Mindy Archeleta, office manager for the law firm that administered the Baker family trusts, responded with genuine warmth. In the years since Lauren and Mike's parents had died, the two women had become friends, occasionally meeting for coffee or lunch, and always taking time away from whatever business Lauren had with the firm to catch up personally.

"I'm fine," Lauren said. "How are you?"

"Crazy busy as always," Mindy said. "But in a good way. Jax is playing Little League this year, can you believe it? It's just T-ball, but he's so stinking cute in his uniform, swinging at the ball. Darrell is helping coach the team, and seeing my two guys together out there on the ball field makes me all gooey inside."

"Send pictures," Lauren said. "I bet little Jax is adorable."

"Darrell looks pretty good in his uniform, too," Mindy said. "Though I'll keep those photos to myself."

Lauren laughed.

"What can I do for you this afternoon?" Mindy asked.

"I wanted to refresh my memory on the terms of the trust," Lauren said. "I'm allowed to draw out money to buy a home, right?"

"You are. Are you thinking of buying a new place?"

Lauren crossed her fingers. Here was where things got a little tricky. "I've been playing around with the idea," she said. "I've seen the place Courtney is interested in and the area is so great. And I'd love to stay close to her and Ashlyn."

"Somewhere in the mountains, right?" Mindy said. "In the southwestern part of the state?"

Adrenaline jolted Lauren, but she managed to keep her voice even. "That's right. Eagle Mountain. I'm here right now. The place is gorgeous."

"Then I guess that request was legit after all," Mindy said.

"What do you mean?" Lauren asked.

"Oh, some man called here last week and asked about getting money from Courtney's trust to buy a ranch out that way. He said he was Courtney's representative. I told him I needed authorization directly from Courtney herself and that we couldn't authorize withdrawals over the phone anyway. Which goes for you, too. You have to come into the office and sign a bunch of papers, and I have to notarize them and everything."

"That's good to know," Lauren said. "Who was the guy? Did he say?"

"He wouldn't give me his name, which is one reason I thought the whole thing was bogus. I mean, you wouldn't believe the scams some people try to pull."

"It was probably her real estate agent, getting ahead of himself," Lauren said.

"Probably. When you talk to Courtney again, tell her we're happy to help her out, but she has to come into the office."

"I will. And thanks for the information, Mindy."

"Anytime. When you get back in town, call me and we'll have lunch. I'll bore you with too many details about Jax's ball games and my own struggles with this new spin class I'm trying. It's supposed to give me a killer bod but so far it just makes me feel inadequate."

"We'll get together soon," Lauren said, and ended the call.

She stood up and began to pace, too agitated to sit still. She'd been right in thinking that Allerton needed Courtney's money to pay for his ranch. He must have been the mysterious "representative" who had called Mindy to ask about withdrawing money from the trust.

She wanted to do a little more digging before she spoke to Shane about this. She needed to make a strong case in order to keep him investigating. She could do a lot on her own, but she really needed—and wanted—his help.

SHANE REPORTED FOR work Thursday morning feeling less than alert. He'd spent a restless night worrying about Lauren. So far, he hadn't seen any evidence that her sister-in-law had done anything other than take up with a perhaps unsuitable man of her own free will. She'd cut contact with everyone for her own reasons, and while that could be a sign of an abusive situation, it also could indicate that she was trying to make a clean break with her old life as Mike Baker's widow and start over again in a new place, with a new man.

But Lauren believed firmly that something was wrong, and Shane wanted to help her. Partly as a way to prove himself as a law enforcement officer, and partly because he was starting to care about this tough but vulnerable woman who was so loyal to her family and so determined to do right by them. And, he had to admit, continuing to investigate this case was a ready-made way to stay close to Lauren, something he very much wanted to do.

He walked into morning roll call to find most of his fellow officers already in place. "Way to go, Ace!" Gage said, and several others applauded.

Shane ignored them and took his seat. "Something tells me our star player hasn't seen the posters for the Fourth of July matchup," Dwight Prentice said. He swiveled his chair and pointed to the bulletin board at the back of the room.

Shane stared at the poster, which featured a shot of him from his playing days, in uniform and grinning at the camera. He leaned closer and suppressed a groan. The photo was the one from his official baseball card the last year he played, taken a few months before he injured his arm. He wore the cocky grin of a man who had the world by the tail and didn't plan on letting go anytime soon.

"Addie says tickets are selling as fast as they can print them," Gage said. "The boys down at the fire station are already whining about how it's not fair for us to bring in a professional."

"I'm not a professional anymore," Shane said. "I'm just a cop."

This brought hoots of laughter from some in the room. Travis, who had been leaning back in his chair observing the banter, cleared his throat and stood, and everyone settled in their seats, facing forward again.

"We've got a few new things to look into this morning," the sheriff said, consulting a clipboard in front of him. "Mountain Aire Boutique filed a shoplifting complaint against Talia Larrivee. The shop's owner, Marsha Raymond, called this morning and said either Talia or one of her friends is robbing her blind and we need to do something to stop it."

"Did she catch them in the act?" Dwight asked.

"No. But she says every time they come into the store, something turns up missing," Travis said.

"Does she have a security camera?" Gage asked. "Maybe she could catch the thefts on film."

"She says she can't put a camera in the changing rooms—her customers would object."

"So no proof, just what she thinks is going on," Gage said. "What did you tell her?"

"I told her we couldn't act on suspicion alone," Travis said. "I told her she had the right to bar Talia and her friends from her shop, but she said she couldn't do that because they spent too much money there."

No one asked why a woman who had the money to afford anything in that shop would steal. For most shoplifters, it was more about getting away with something than getting an item for free. For some people, it was a compulsion; for others, a cheap thrill.

"This isn't the first time someone has complained about Talia being light-fingered," Dwight said. "But no one has been able to catch her in the act."

"Someone caught her one time," Gage said. "Over at the hardware store. Fred Wilkins was red-hot about it, too, but Talia's daddy showed up to pay for the items she stole and smooth Fred's feathers."

"More like grease Fred's palm," Dwight said.

"In any case, if you see Talia shopping in town, it

wouldn't hurt to keep an eye on her and her friends," Travis said. "But be subtle. We don't want any complaints of harassment." He consulted the clipboard again. "Shane, where are you on that welfare check on Courtney Baker?"

Shane sat up straighter. "I tracked Courtney Baker and her companion's movements. They were registered at the Ranch Motel as Mr. and Mrs. Troy Allen. Trey Allerton and another man, whose name I don't have—Allerton introduced him as his business partner—struck a deal with Samuel Russell to lease a section of Russell's ranch for five years. Russell said Courtney visited the ranch with Russell, his business partner, and another woman I haven't been able to identify. I visited the property with Lauren Baker, Courtney's sister-in-law, and in an abandoned mobile home on the property, we found a doll Lauren said belonged to her niece, Ashlyn. I haven't learned anything more."

"Have you found any indication of foul play or anything illegal?" Travis asked.

"No, sir. Registering at the motel under a false name is suspicious, but it's not against the law."

"We'll keep our ears open, but I don't hear anything in what you've told us that sounds like a crime."

"No, sir. Lauren thinks her sister-in-law is acting out of character, but Mr. Russell said she didn't seem distressed when he saw her, and the clerk at the motel says the same."

"Brenda rented her old apartment to Lauren," Dwight said. "She thinks her concern for her sister-in-law and niece is legitimate, for what it's worth."

"Concern isn't enough for us to launch a full investigation," Travis said.

"I'd like to continue to follow up on this in my spare time," Shane said. "I'd like to find out more about the other couple who were with Allerton and Mrs. Baker at the Russell Ranch."

"That's fine," Travis said. "But don't make it a priority." He consulted the clipboard again. "Item number three…"

Shane forced himself to pay attention to the details of ongoing cases, a couple of BOLOs that had come in overnight and some housekeeping issues they needed to address. By the time the meeting ended, he had largely put Courtney Baker out of his mind.

But when he returned to his desk, he was startled—and pleased—to find Lauren Baker waiting for him. She stood as he approached. "Adelaide told me I could wait here for you."

"I see you're on a first-name basis with our office manager," Shane said.

"She insisted," Lauren said.

He settled behind the desk. "It's always good to see you."

She sat also, but her hands remained restless, clutching at the purse in her lap, or reaching up to smooth her hair. "Is something wrong?" he asked.

"I've found something," she said. "Maybe something important. Trey Allerton tried to get money from Courtney's trust."

He pulled out a notebook so he could make notes. "How did you find this out?" he asked.

She told him about calling the law firm that managed the trust and chatting up her friend, the office manager. "I checked Courtney's bank, too. Her checking account has been emptied, but that happened three weeks ago. Her savings account still has a little in it, but that money hasn't been touched."

"That information has to be confidential," he said. "How did you find it out?"

She flushed. "I told you I did Courtney's taxes last year, right? She gave me her online passwords so I could download all the transactions into my online accounting software. I told her she should change the passwords after I was done, but she never did."

"So she took money out of her checking account," he said. "How much money?"

"Less than a thousand dollars."

"How much is in savings?"

"About five thousand. There are some other accounts—a college fund for Ashlyn, a medical savings account and a retirement account. They're with a different bank and I wasn't able to check them."

"You didn't have the passwords?"

"They require a new password every three months."

He suppressed a grin. Clearly, Lauren had tried to hack into those accounts and been thwarted. He admired her determination, if not the not-exactly-legal approach to gathering information.

"This is all very interesting," he said. "But it doesn't prove that anything is wrong."

She scooted to the edge of her chair and leaned toward him. "Why did Allerton—or whoever the man was—call the trust fund to inquire about withdrawing money, and not Courtney herself?" she asked. "And why didn't Courtney follow up on the request for the money? Was it because she had refused to do so? Or because she couldn't?"

Chapter Seven

Shane had no answer for Lauren's question as to why Courtney had never followed up on the request to withdraw money from her trust fund. He had asked her to share anything else she learned, and promised to keep searching for more information about Courtney and Ashlyn and Trey Allerton. But she heard the reluctance behind the promise. He didn't really believe Courtney was in trouble.

Lauren wasn't going to give up, though. Thursday afternoon, she walked to the Eagle Mountain Medical Clinic. A dark-haired woman at the front counter greeted her. "Hello. Do you have an appointment?"

"I'm Lauren Baker, from Denver," she said. "I'm a nurse practitioner, and I wondered if I could speak to the clinic director for a moment." She handed over one of her business cards.

The woman—her name tag identified her as Rebecca—stood. "I'll see if Ms. Cox is free."

Lauren took a seat in the waiting room. Across from her, an elderly couple flipped through magazines. Next to them, a woman cradled a fussy toddler. The room was simply furnished, the chairs and tables slightly worn, but the magazines were of recent issue and everything was clean. It looked like a typical busy clinic, one that devoted funding to patient services rather than decorating, probably because there wasn't excess funding to go around.

"Ms. Baker?" A middle-aged woman with short dark hair streaked with silver, dressed in a navy pantsuit, approached.

Lauren stood. "I'm Lauren Baker."

"Linda Cox." She offered her hand. "Let's go into my office."

Ms. Cox led the way to a small office crowded with a desk, one visitor's chair and a row of filing cabinets. "What can I do for you, Ms. Baker?" she asked.

"I'm looking for this woman and her little girl." She passed over the photograph of Courtney and Ashlyn. "That's my late brother's widow, Courtney Baker, and her daughter, Ashlyn. They've been missing for several weeks now. The last anyone heard from them, they were in Eagle Mountain. I wondered if either of them had been seen in your clinic."

Ms. Cox studied the picture for a moment, then laid it on the desk between them. "As a nurse practitioner, you're aware that patient information is confidential."

Lauren tightened her hands on the arms of the chair. "I'm not asking you to divulge particulars, or anything about a medical condition," she said. "I'm only asking if they were seen at this clinic. I'm trying to track their whereabouts."

"Have you consulted the sheriff's department about this?" Ms. Cox asked.

"I have. But they tell me they can't devote much time to the search if there's no evidence of a crime having been committed. But I know Courtney. She wouldn't have cut off communication with me and with everyone else she knows if something wasn't wrong."

Ms. Cox stood and picked up the photograph. "Give me a moment."

Lauren clenched her hands in her lap and tried to focus on taking deep, slow breaths. She reminded herself that if Ashlyn and Courtney hadn't been seen at the clinic, it meant they were well, which was a good thing. But if they had been seen, it would be one more clue to what they had been doing here—and with whom.

Ms. Cox returned to the office, along with a young African American woman. "This is Tina, Dr. Folsom's nurse. She helped care for your niece when she was here two weeks ago," Ms. Cox said. "She can't give you any medical information, but there may be other questions she can answer."

Lauren stood, heart beating fast. "Ashlyn was here? Was her mother, Courtney, with her?"

Tina nodded. "Her mother was with her, and a man. I wasn't sure what his relation to them was, and he didn't say."

"What did the man look like?" Lauren asked.

Tina frowned. "He was white, with brown hair. Kind of tall." She shrugged. "It's been a while, and my focus was on the patient."

Lauren longed to ask what was wrong with Ashlyn.

Why had she been seen? But confidentiality rules prevented the clinic from providing any of those details. "How did they seem?" she asked. "I mean, were they relaxed or nervous? Did they seem afraid of the man or comfortable with him?"

"The woman was concerned about her daughter, but not unduly so. And she didn't seem afraid, no." She glanced at Ms. Cox. "Was this some kind of abusive situation and I missed it?"

"Was it?" Ms. Cox asked.

"No," Lauren said. At least, Trey had never shown any sign of violence toward Courtney or Ashlyn, but that might have changed. "But it didn't strike you that she was trying to get away from him or anything?"

Tina shook her head. "She and I were alone in the exam room with the little girl before the doctor came in. The man stayed in the waiting room. If she had wanted to say anything to me, or to Dr. Folsom, she could have."

"Did she mention where they were going after they left the clinic?" Lauren asked.

"Not that I remember."

"Was Ashlyn going to be okay?"

Tina looked to Ms. Cox again. The director nodded. "She was going to be fine," Tina said. "It wasn't anything serious."

"Thank you," Lauren said.

"You can go back to work now, Tina," Ms. Cox said.

When they were alone again, Ms. Cox said, "Was that helpful?"

"It verifies they were still in town then," Lauren said. "And that they were okay." That was all good, but it didn't tell her why Courtney didn't answer calls or texts or post to social media.

Ms. Cox closed the door leading to the hallway. "Now I have a question for you," she said.

"All right," Lauren said.

"Would you be interested in moving to Eagle Mountain, to work for us?"

Lauren blinked, taken aback. "Nothing like that ever crossed my mind."

"Think about it," Ms. Cox said. "When you walked in and gave your card to Rebecca, I thought you had heard through the grapevine that we were looking to add a nurse practitioner. I hoped you had come to apply for the job."

"I'm very flattered," Lauren said. "But I'm happy where I am."

"If that changes, give me a call." Ms. Cox handed over her own card. "We have a good practice here, lots of variety and a good team. And Eagle Mountain is a wonderful place to live. I'm happy to provide more details anytime."

"Thank you." Lauren stood. "And thank you for telling me about Courtney."

"I hope you find your friend and your niece," she said. "If I hear anything else about them, I'll let you know."

"Thank you."

Lauren left the clinic and was walking back toward her rental when a familiar voice hailed her. Shane pulled his sheriff's department SUV to the curb beside her. "You look like you just lost your best friend," he said.

"I dropped by the medical clinic," she said. "Ashlyn was seen there two weeks ago."

His look of genuine concern touched her. "What happened?"

"Confidentiality laws prevented them from telling me any details, but they assured me she's going to be okay. She was seen for something minor."

"Then why do you look so down?"

She hugged her arms across her stomach. "The nurse who took care of Ashlyn said Trey was with them. He stayed in the waiting room while Courtney and Ashlyn went back. It was the perfect opportunity for Courtney to ask for help if she needed it but the nurse said she seemed fine."

"That's good," he said. "Isn't it?"

"It is—but if everything was going so well, why did she stop returning calls and texts from everyone she knew back in Denver? And why did she stop posting on all her social media?"

"I don't know," he said. "You want to get coffee somewhere? I'd like to keep talking, but I'm holding up traffic."

She realized two other vehicles were patiently idling behind his SUV. "Sure," she said, and climbed in.

"Did you learn anything else at the clinic?" he asked as he pulled in to the flow of traffic once more.

"Not really. But they offered me a job. Apparently, they want to add a nurse practitioner."

"Are you going to take the offer?"

"No. I'm happy where I am." She'd been at the clinic in Denver for five years. Like any job, it had its drawbacks, but overall it was a very good position. She had no reason to want to change.

"You mind if I ask a nosy question?"

"Isn't that what cops do?"

He chuckled. "We do. You don't have to answer if you don't want to, but if you have this big trust fund from your family, what are you doing working as a nurse?"

"A nurse practitioner. I enjoy my work. I'd never be comfortably living off my parents' money. And what about you?"

"What about me?" he asked.

"I looked you up online. You made a lot of money when you played professional ball."

"And paid a lot of taxes and blew a lot on expensive vacations and gifts for family and friends."

"So you blew it all?"

"Not all of it. I had smart people who talked me into investing some. And I have a house."

"A house in Eagle Mountain?"

"Yeah. Would you like to see it?"

"Yes," she said, surprising herself with the answer. "Yes, I would."

Shane had purchased his house while he was still pitching, thinking he would use it as a retreat during the off-season, or a place to stay when he came home to visit family. He had retreated here, all right—to recover after his surgery, and again when he had been released from his contract and officially retired from the only job he had ever really wanted to do.

He pulled in to the driveway and cut the engine and waited for Lauren to say something. The log cabin, with its twin dormers and broad front porch, sat in the shade of tall spruce trees. It was large, but it wasn't elaborate or modern, or even very new. "It's not what I expected," she said.

"You thought I'd have some modern mansion, or a swinging bachelor pad." He'd heard similar comments before.

She flushed. "I guess so."

"Come on. I'll show you around."

He led the way along a flagstone path, up the steps and across the porch. She stopped to stroke the arm of a wooden rocker. "This is beautiful."

"I got it from a local guy who makes handmade furniture."

The front door led directly into a great room, which took up most of the downstairs. Light poured from large windows on all sides, onto wood plank flooring. He'd furnished the room with comfortable leather furniture, a large entertainment center and a wall of bookcases. A dining table and chairs from the craftsman who had made the rocking chair filled one side of the space, in front of the island that separated the kitchen area. "There's a master suite through there," he said, pointing to a hallway off the living area. "And three more bedrooms and two baths upstairs."

Her gaze fixed on him, a softness in her expression that made him feel shaky inside. "What?" he asked.

"You didn't buy a house," she said. "You bought a family home."

He shrugged. "I'd like to have a family—one day."

He led the way back over toward the seating area. "Did I hear right that you're from Eagle Mountain?" she asked.

"That's right," he said. "I went to high school here. My mom and dad live across town."

"Do you have any brothers or sisters?" she asked.

He settled onto the sofa, and she perched on the adjacent love seat. "I have a sister. She's in Minneapolis."

"Why did you decide to come back here instead of staying in Denver?" she asked. "I assume that's where you lived when you played."

"I had an apartment there, but I guess I'm not much of a city guy. I like the mountains and the woods. And I hated Denver traffic."

"I guess no one likes the traffic," she said.

"What about you?" he asked. "Are you from Denver originally?"

She shook her head. "Lincoln, Nebraska. But I've lived in Denver for almost five years."

"Do you like it?"

"I do. Not the traffic, but I have a nice apartment close to work, and I really enjoy my job."

"It's good to have work you enjoy."

"Do you enjoy your work? Being a sheriff's deputy is very different from playing professional baseball."

He leaned his head back against the sofa and looked up at the ceiling. "When the club decided not to renew my contract, my whole world changed." He hadn't talked much about that time, but he found himself wanting to tell her. "I'd never thought about being anything but a ballplayer. Shortsighted of me, I guess, but when you're on top, you think you'll never fall."

"That must have been hard."

He shrugged. "I was upset, but I was only twenty-eight. I had to figure out something to do with the rest of my life. I saw that the sheriff's department here was hiring, so I did a ride-along."

"What drew you to that choice?" she asked.

He'd heard variations of that question before, usually phrased along the lines of "Why would you want to be a cop?" said with a tinge of horror. "It's nothing like what you see on TV, all excitement and danger and everything," he said. "I mean, you train for that stuff, but most of the time it's interacting with people, keeping an eye out for trouble and helping people out. I liked that. I wanted to be a part of the community again, to do something that really made people's lives better. I know some law enforcement get a bad rap and there have been problems other places, but this is a good group of officers here. It seems like a good fit, though I guess I'm still finding my footing."

"People like you," she said. "And people in town are proud of you. Everyone I've talked to has good things to say about you."

A familiar regret pulled at him. "They're proud of what I was."

"I don't know about that." She tilted her head, letting her gaze sweep over him. "All the women in town think you're pretty hot stuff."

He let out a hoot of laughter. "You're one to talk. I've already had three men ask about you."

"You're kidding!"

"I'm not. You have to remember that men still out-number women in a lot of small towns out here. Some-one new always sparks interest. Dating in a small town is risky because you can run through all the potential partners pretty quickly."

She looked amused. "And have you run through all the potential partners?"

"I'll never tell." He stood. "I need to change out of this uniform, then how about I fix us something to eat? I skipped lunch and I'm starved."

"All right."

"Feel free to look around more if you want."

Shedding the utility belt, weapon and ballistics vest lightened him by ten pounds and was always a relief. He thought about taking a quick shower, but settled for sponging off and changing into jeans and a T-shirt. When he returned to the great room, Lauren was stand-ing in front of the bookcase. "You like detective nov-els," she said by way of greeting.

"Real-life crimes are seldom as easy to solve, but I've always liked figuring out puzzles." He moved to the kitchen. "Grilled chicken okay?" he asked.

"Sounds good." She moved to the other side of the island and watched as he unwrapped chicken thighs and mixed up a quick marinade. When he took out salad greens, she said, "You still eat like an athlete."

"I still have to stay in shape," he said.

"Have you ever had to chase down a criminal?"

"I chased a shoplifter down Main just a couple of

weeks ago. A teenager. I think he was surprised an old guy like me caught him."

She laughed. "I saw a poster for a baseball game on the Fourth of July," she said. "Sherriff's department versus fire department. There was a picture of you in your Rockies uniform."

"I've been drafted to pitch for our side." He tore lettuce and added it to a bowl. "Apparently, the sheriff's team has lost to the fire department for the past four years and I'm supposed to stop the slide."

"No pressure."

He sent her a grateful look. "Everyone still thinks I'm the pro ace, but if I was, I'd still be on the mound, not sitting in a cruiser."

Her gaze shifted to his arm, and the scar that wrapped around his elbow, white against his tan. "Does it hurt to pitch?"

"It hurt to throw the ball as hard and fast, and for as long, as I needed to do in the majors." He began slicing a bell pepper. "But I can pitch to a bunch of amateurs. It just won't be the spectacle people seem to expect."

"I wouldn't know the difference, and I'll bet a lot of other people are the same." She slid onto a bar stool. "I'd offer to help you with dinner, but you look like you've got everything under control."

"I do." He pulled out a tomato and began cutting it into chunks, and decided it was past time to shift the conversation away from himself. "Besides visiting the clinic, what else did you do today?"

"I followed up on some rental referrals and found a place that agreed to rent to me week to week for as long as I want. I'll move in tomorrow," she said. "I don't have to be out of the Prentices' place until Monday morning, but this way Brenda can rent her apartment out for the weekend. Apparently, there's a big demand."

"How did you luck into your new place on such short notice?"

"It's not a regular rental," she said. "It's a detached cottage where the owner's mother lived until she had to go into an assisted living facility last month. She wants to fix it up and rent it out but hadn't gotten around to it yet. But Mallory talked her into letting me have it, as long as I'm not picky, which I'm not."

"Then it sounds like a win for everyone." He picked up the bowl of chicken. "Come on outside."

While the chicken grilled, she helped him set the table on the patio. They ate grilled chicken and salad and drank iced tea. When they had finished, she walked to the deck railing and looked out at his view of a wooded valley.

"It is beautiful here," she said.

"I like it." He joined her at the railing, close, but not quite touching. He caught the scent of her perfume, something floral with a hint of citrus. Feminine and stirring.

"I don't just mean your house, I mean the whole area."

"Thousands of tourists can't be wrong."

She turned toward him. "But is beautiful scenery enough? It's great for a vacation, but to live your whole life?"

"I guess that depends on what you value, what fulfills you. That isn't the same for every person. And the answer isn't the same throughout a person's life. But for me, right now, it's enough."

"You don't think you're missing out on some things?"

Should he be glib or honest? He chose honesty. "Someone to share it with, maybe. If I had that, I think this would be just about perfect."

"I think that could make almost anything perfect," she said. "If you found the right person."

Their eyes met, and he felt a pull somewhere around his heart. There was something about this woman that caught and held him, not like a trap, but more like a warm embrace. Did she feel it, too? He moved closer and put his hand on her shoulder. She continued to look steadily into his eyes, almost daring him to move in nearer still.

So he did. She tilted her head up in invitation, and his lips met hers in a slow, sweet kiss that sent heat spreading through him.

Her fingers gripped his shoulder, a gentle, insistent pressure, and he wrapped his arms around her, their bodies pressed together, soft to hard, curve to plain.

Then she was moving away again, easing out of his arms, her face flushed, her breathing a little shallow. "That was nice," he said.

"Yes." She looked around, everywhere but at him. "But I think I'd better go now."

His first impulse was to tell her she didn't have to go, but he thought better of it. "I'll get my keys."

They were silent on the drive back to her rental. He

parked out front and unfastened his seat belt. "You don't have to get out," she said.

"I'll walk you to your door," he said, not leaving room for argument.

At the door, he waited while she dug out her key. "Thank you for dinner," she said.

"Thank you," he said. "You're good company."

"So are you."

"About that kiss," he began.

"You don't have to apologize."

"I wasn't going to apologize. I enjoyed it. A lot. And I wouldn't mind repeating it sometime. But I didn't want it hanging between us, if it made you feel awkward or pressured or…whatever."

At last, she looked at him again. "It was a good kiss," she said. "I'm just not interested in starting something when I'm not going to stick around. I'm here to find Courtney and Ashlyn, and then I'm going back to Denver."

"Denver isn't so far away," he said.

"I know." She bit her lower lip. "I have a bad habit."

He waited, but when she didn't say more, he prompted. "What is it? Do you bite your nails? Are you a closet smoker?"

A smile flirted with the corners of her mouth. "I have a bad habit of falling for men. Falling too hard, too soon. It's…awkward when things don't work out."

Was she saying she was falling for him? The idea made him a little light-headed. He brushed his hand down her arm. "It was a nice kiss," he said. "I'm not expecting more. You don't have to, either."

She nodded. "But I think we should stick to looking for Courtney."

"All right." That was a reason for him to see her again. As for the rest—he might not have expectations, but he could hope. It was a subtle difference, but one he could build on. And if they fell, maybe they could do it together.

Chapter Eight

The next day Lauren moved to her new rental. She did laundry and paid a few bills, filling her time with these mundane tasks to avoid thinking too much about Shane and the kiss they had shared.

It had been a good kiss. The kind she'd like to repeat. The time she had spent at his house, having dinner and getting to know each other, had been some of the best hours she'd had since Mike died. She really liked Shane, but that worried her. She'd fallen too hard and fast for men before, and the breakups had really hurt. She didn't want to go through that pain again.

She was still pondering all this when her phone rang in late afternoon. She didn't recognize the number. "Hello?" she answered, prepared to hang up on a telemarketer.

"Lauren? It's Mindy, from Addison, Simmons and Clark."

"Mindy!" Lauren relaxed. "What can I do for you?"

"I'm not at work and I'm calling from my personal phone, so this isn't an official call," Mindy said. "I probably shouldn't even be talking to you about this, but I'm worried."

Lauren perched on the arm of the floral sofa in the rental. "What's wrong?" she asked. "What are you worried about?"

"Courtney called the office this morning."

Lauren stood again, too agitated to sit. "Is she all right? Did she say where she was calling from?"

"Don't you know where she is?" Mindy asked.

Lauren remembered that she hadn't told Mindy that Courtney was missing. "I haven't seen her in several weeks," she said. "She left town and hasn't been answering my calls or texts. I've been worried sick about her."

"Now I'm even more concerned," Mindy said.

"Why did she call you?" Lauren asked.

"She wanted money from her trust. But not for a house purchase. She said she needed it for medical bills for Ashlyn. And then she started crying."

Lauren's stomach clenched. "What did she say was wrong with Ashlyn?"

"She didn't say. At least not to me. I was hoping you'd know."

"This is the first I've heard about Ashlyn being ill. She was fine when I saw her last." She took a deep breath, trying to rein in her emotions and think logically. "How much money did she ask for?"

"She said she needed ten thousand dollars right away. Mr. Simmons talked to her and said he'd arrange for the funds to be made available. You really don't know anything about this?"

"No." The clinic here in Eagle Mountain had said Ashlyn's visit to them wasn't for anything serious. Had it turned out to be serious after all? "Can you find out where she wanted the money sent?"

"That's supposed to be confidential information," Mindy said. "You know that."

"This could be really important," Lauren said. "I don't trust the man she was hanging out with before she left Denver. I need to find her and make sure she's all right."

"I'm not supposed to snoop, but I'll admit I did," Mindy said. "I was that concerned about her. You won't tell anyone where you got this information, will you?"

"Not a soul," Lauren promised.

"All right, then. I looked on the computer and she requested the money be wired to a bank in Telluride."

Telluride was only about an hour from Eagle Mountain. So Courtney was still in the area. "Did she leave an address for where she's staying, or information on how to get in touch with her?"

"If she did, it's not in her computer file. And I can't snoop around on Mr. Simmons's desk. I don't want to lose my job."

"Thanks for letting me know all this," Lauren said. "I really appreciate it."

"Let me know what you find out," Mindy said. "I hope Ashlyn is okay."

"I hope so, too." They said goodbye and Lauren sank onto the sofa, feeling hollowed out. Mindy had said Courtney was crying. Her sister-in-law wasn't one to fake something like that. She wasn't manipulative or in the habit of lying to get her way.

She took out her phone and studied it a minute. She

had thought it would be a good idea to stay away from Shane for a few days, to give them both time to cool off a little. But she needed his help now. She dialed his cell phone and listened to it ring. After five buzzing rings, a mechanical voice transferred her to Shane's mailbox. "Courtney contacted the trust fund administrator and asked for ten thousand dollars to be wired to a bank in Telluride," Lauren said. "She told them she needed the money for Ashlyn's medical bills. How can we find out where they are, and if Ashlyn is okay?"

She hung up, fighting down panic. Fear gripped her—fear for her niece, and for Courtney. She had promised Mike she would look out for his widow and his little girl, but right now she was failing miserably.

"Come on, Shane, you're gonna show those smoke breathers what real heat feels like!"

"Whoo, Shane! Smoke 'em!"

Shane gave a half-hearted grin and walked toward the mound on the high school baseball field at this first official practice Friday evening, which a number of people had gathered to watch. Baseball wasn't a first-tier sport in a mountain town, where even June games could be snowed out and spring training often had to be moved indoors because of cold weather, and the field showed it. A family of ground squirrels had colonized left field, and the chalk lines for the bases ran over clumps of weeds.

Then again, the players weren't professional level, either, ranging in age from nineteen to fifty, the latter being a reserve deputy who had bragged that he had been a pretty good player back in college. A few decades and many cheeseburgers ago, Shane thought.

Dwight was catching, and fired the ball to Shane on the mound. Shane rubbed it up, the familiar feel of leather comforting. He wound up and hurled a strike over the plate. The crowd applauded and whistled. They were easily impressed, since Shane hadn't even put much energy behind that first warm-up toss. He tossed a few more, gaining confidence. Dwight pantomimed a stinging hand and gave Shane a thumbs-up. "I'm ready," Shane said. "Let's get this show on the road."

The sheriff strode to the batting box and assumed his stance. "Whatever you do, don't hit him!" someone on the sidelines called, and everyone around him laughed.

Shane pitched a strike and Travis didn't move. "Strike one!" the umpire—Bud O'Brien, owner of the local garage—called.

Travis fouled off the next pitch, then Shane threw a ball. He ended up striking out the sheriff, and the next two batters. As he walked off the mound, the spectators cheered. "You looked great out there," Gage said, and slapped him on the back.

"How's your arm?" Dwight asked.

"It's fine," Shane said. "It feels good." It had felt exhilarating out on that dirt mound, too, looking down on the batter's box, cleats digging in as he executed his windup. But it felt a little like cheating, too. Pitching to most of these guys was like pitching to Little Leaguers. He didn't have to bring his best stuff to beat them.

Which was just as well, his ego reminded him. Because his best stuff was long gone.

Gage took over pitching for the next group of batters. He didn't have Shane's speed, but he was pretty accurate, and though fireman Al Tomlinson hit a high fly, Deputy Jamie Douglas caught the ball and fired it back to first.

Shane turned his attention from the game to the crowd filling the rickety bleachers. "Hey, Shane!" Taylor Redmond called and waved to him.

He nodded and looked past her to another group of women. Talia Larrivee and her posse. With a thick-set man with a moustache whom Shane didn't recognize.

Adelaide sidled over to him and followed his gaze to the bleachers. "Who are you looking for?" she asked.

"Nobody," he lied. He had hoped Lauren might show up to watch the practice, but why should she? It sounded as if she didn't follow baseball, and he wasn't sure how she felt about him since that kiss. She had liked the kiss, and she had wanted it at the time, but afterward, she'd been upset. Whether because she had decided she didn't like him that much, or she liked him too much, he wasn't sure.

"Who's that with Talia Larrivee?" he asked.

Adelaide squinted. "I don't know, but I can find out."

"Adelaide, no!"

But she ignored him and made a beeline for the bleachers. A moment later, she stood in front of the couple. The man looked from Adelaide to Shane. He was too far away to clearly make out his expression, but Shane was pretty sure the man wasn't too happy to know a deputy had been asking about him.

Adelaide made her way back to Shane. "He told me

his name was none of my business, but right before I got to them, I heard Talia address him as Tom."

"Next time you should be more subtle," Shane said.

"Why? Sometimes the direct approach gets the best results."

"Shane! You're up!"

He headed for the mound, pushing aside thoughts of the mysterious Tom, or Lauren or anyone else.

Two hours later, practice ended and he headed for his house to shower and eat whatever he could find in the refrigerator. He'd turned down an offer to go out with a couple of his teammates, not eager to deal with the crowd of locals who had gathered around to congratulate him. They all wanted to talk about his days as a player, and that wasn't history he cared to relive.

He started to undress, and when he pulled out his phone, he saw that he had missed a call from Lauren. Surprised, and pleased, he punched the code for his voice mail.

"Courtney contacted the trust fund administrator." Tension stretched Lauren's voice and his chest tightened as the message continued. "How can we find out where she is and if Ashlyn is all right?"

He punched in Lauren's number. "I got your message," he said when she answered. "I'll be over in a few minutes and we'll talk about this."

Chapter Nine

Twenty minutes later, Shane was at the door of Lauren's rental. His hair was damp, curling at his temples, and he smelled of soap. "Did I pull you out of the shower?" she asked.

"I had just finished ball practice."

"How did it go?"

He took her hand and squeezed it, his touch gentle and reassuring. "It went fine, but you didn't call me to talk about baseball. What's going on with Courtney?"

"My friend at the lawyer's office called to tell me Courtney got in touch with them. But please don't tell anyone that's how I heard about this. My friend could get into real trouble for breaking a client's confidentiality. She could lose her job."

"I don't see any need to bring her into this," he said. "At least, not now." He led her over to the sofa, the floral upholstery something his grandmother might have owned. "Let's sit down and you can tell me everything. Something about the call concerned your friend enough that she got in touch with you."

Lauren nodded and sat, her hands fisted in her lap.

"Courtney said she needed ten thousand dollars right away to pay medical bills for Ashlyn. But the nurse at the clinic here in town said they saw Ashlyn for something minor. And she's always been a healthy child. But what if she's been in an accident, or she has cancer or something?" She swallowed tears. Now that Shane was here, she was on the verge of giving in to the wild fears that ricocheted through her.

"Isn't Ashlyn covered by medical insurance?" he asked.

The question was like a stiff breeze clearing away fog. "Yes," she said. "She and Courtney are both covered by the military's health insurance—Courtney until she remarries, and Ashlyn until she's twenty-one." She shook her head. "I don't know why I didn't think of it before."

"I can't think of any situation where a medical facility would demand ten thousand dollars before they would treat Ashlyn," he said. "So Courtney wasn't telling the truth why she needed the money."

Lauren sagged with relief. "So Ashlyn probably isn't sick."

"I don't think so," he said. "I think Courtney made up that story—or maybe Allerton or someone else made it up and convinced her to call and ask for the money, after their first attempt to get cash from her trust failed."

"I don't know how much the man who called before asked for from the trust," she said. "But he said it was to buy a house, and that would cost hundreds of thousands. Why ask for only ten thousand this time?"

"That's the amount of the payment Trey Allerton

owes Sam Russell for the lease," Shane said. "Did your friend indicate whether or not the lawyer agreed to send the money?"

"I'm not sure she knows," Lauren said. "I was so upset I forgot to ask. But the information about a bank in Telluride, where Courtney wanted the money sent, was in the file, so that may mean they were going to send it. And I'll bet the lawyer got her contact information, too—a telephone number where he could reach her, and maybe an address, too."

"It would be helpful if your friend could pass that information to us."

Lauren shook her head. "She says it's not in the file, and she's too afraid of losing her job if she's caught snooping in the senior partner's office. But you could find out."

He frowned. "How am I supposed to do that?"

"If you call and say you're searching for Courtney, that she's a missing person, don't they have to give you whatever information they have?" But the look on his face—somewhere between pity and frustration—told her she was wrong.

He raked one hand through his hair. "Look. No attorney is going to reveal information about a client without a warrant requiring him to do so. And no judge is going to authorize a warrant without probable cause that a crime has been committed."

"What kind of proof?"

"A threat. A cry for help. Some evidence that Courtney is in real danger."

"Everything about this situation is wrong," she said.

"Courtney and I are friends. We're like sisters. She's closer to me than she is to any of her blood relatives. She wouldn't disappear like this unless she was in big trouble."

"I believe you," he said. "But it's not enough for a judge."

"Courtney wouldn't lie," she said. "She's the daughter of a preacher, and she's the most honest person I know." Her stomach hurt. "So someone either forced her to say those things to the lawyer, or Ashlyn really is ill."

"I don't think Ashlyn is ill," he said. "Do you think Allerton could persuade her to lie for him?"

"I don't know. I don't want to believe it, but if he threatened her or Ashlyn…" She shook her head, not wanting to finish the thought.

"Sometimes people will do uncharacteristic things for people they think they're in love with," he said.

"Courtney isn't in love with Trey Allerton."

"She might believe she is." The gentleness in his voice and his eyes didn't soften the blow of his words. "She's a young woman. She's probably lonely. You've said Allerton came across as charming. He's good-looking. He paid her a lot of attention. She wouldn't be the first person to be taken in under those circumstances."

"I don't believe it. Courtney can be very naive and trusting, but she's not stupid." But was she refusing to believe Courtney had real feelings for Allerton because that was true—or because admitting the possibility felt like a betrayal of her brother? "If you can't get a warrant to get Courtney's contact information from her lawyer, what can you do?" she asked.

He was silent for a long moment, then he said, "I'd

like to talk to Samuel Russell again. If he's received the ten thousand dollars Allerton owes, it isn't proof the money came from Courtney, but it is suspicious. And I should speak to any neighbors in the area. Maybe one of them saw or heard something that will give us a clue about the nature of Courtney's relationship with Allerton. I'd also like to find out more about the other couple Sam Russell saw with Courtney and Allerton."

Her spirits lifted a little. "Those are all good ideas," she said. "What can I do to help?"

"Check in with other family and friends and see if Courtney has contacted any of them in the last week or so. I'll let you know what I find out, but don't expect to hear anything right away. I have to do my investigating when I'm off-duty. This isn't an official case."

"Because we don't know if a crime has really been committed," she said. "I get it." She buried her face in her hands, overwhelmed. "I feel so helpless. And I'm worried if we take too long to find them, Courtney or Ashlyn could end up hurt."

"Do you think Allerton is violent?" he asked.

"I think he could be. I just don't know." To her horror, she started to cry. She jumped up, trying to choke back the tears, but Shane stood also and pulled her into his arms.

"It's okay," he said. "We're going to find them."

She gave in to the sobs, great waves of them. She hadn't wept like this since the weeks right after Mike died. Amid the storm of emotion, she was aware of Shane's strong arms encircling her, of his strong shoulders supporting her. She smelled the clean cotton of the shirt she was soaking with her tears, and felt the soft brush of his lips against her hair. She wanted to cling to him, reveling in the comfort and security of his touch, letting his strength make her stronger. How long had it been since she had felt so cared for?

But was it real affection driving those feelings, or only her need? Doubt was like a burr under her clothes, a distraction she didn't welcome. She pulled away and wiped at her eyes with her fingers. "I'll be okay," she said. "You should go. You must be tired after working all day, then playing baseball."

"It was just a practice," he said. "I'm fine. I can stay awhile longer."

She sniffed and forced a smile. "Really, I'm okay."

He looked as if he wanted to argue but apparently decided against it. "Call me if you need anything. Anytime. I mean it, understand?"

She nodded, and the smile was genuine this time. "Thanks for coming over. Talking to you—and knowing you're going to help—means a lot." She leaned in and kissed him—on the cheek, the rasp of beard stubble against her lips sending a jolt of heat through her.

His eyes met hers, and for the briefest moment she glimpsed how much he wanted her, and she caught her breath. Then he turned away. "We'll talk tomorrow," he said, and left. But she remained frozen in place for a long time, stunned by the strength of his feelings for her—and by her own desire for him.

SAMUEL RUSSELL WELCOMED Shane into his kitchen the next morning. The rancher didn't remark on the early hour—just after eight, but the older man had probably been up hours. In Shane's experience, farmers and ranchers rose at first light or before, in order to do all the work living on the land required. "How about some coffee?" Russell asked as he led the way into a kitchen that looked untouched since the 1970s.

"That would be great." Shane wore jeans and a Rayford County Sheriff's Department T-shirt. He didn't go on duty until three and hoped to learn as much as he could from Russell and his neighbors before then.

Russell brought two mugs of coffee to the square wooden table and sat, and motioned for Shane to do the same. "What can I do for you?" he asked.

Shane cautiously sipped the coffee. It was hot and strong and exactly what he needed. "Have you heard from Trey Allerton or his partner?" he asked.

"Yep." Russell blew on his coffee, then sipped. "Yesterday I got a check for ten thousand dollars." He set down the mug. "To tell you the truth, it surprised me. I haven't seen them around in a few days, so I figured the whole lot might have skipped town."

"Have you seen them since you received the payment?" Shane asked.

Russell shook his head. "Not a whisker."

"Is there anyone else living around here, maybe a neighbor who might have seen or talked to them?"

"You might talk to Robby and Becca Olsen," Russell said. "They have the property on the other side of the piece I leased to Allen and his bunch. They moved out here about a year ago from some city up north and said they were going to live off the land. I thought they'd last maybe a couple of months, but they're still sticking with it. I'll say one thing for them—they aren't afraid of hard work. They built a yurt, of all things, and put up a big greenhouse, got chickens and goats and pigs and who knows what else. I still think it's crazy, but they're nice enough, for all their odd ideas."

Shane finished his coffee, then went in search of the Olsens. He found them setting fence posts around a trio of beehives a few hundred yards from a forest green canvas yurt surrounded by a wood deck. Robby Olsen hailed Shane when he got out of his pickup. "Come on back!" he shouted, then went back to pounding in steel posts.

Shane walked past a chicken house and chicken yard, a pigpen where two very large spotted hogs grunted at him, and a plastic-covered greenhouse three times the size of the yurt. The purple-and-yellow beehives stood out amid the sunburnt grass where they had been situated, and as Shane neared, he heard a low hum from the hives and saw bees filling the air around them.

A young man in cargo shorts and no shirt stepped forward and offered his hand. "I'm Robby Olsen," he said. "Mr. Russell called and said you were coming to see us."

"I'm Becca." The woman, tall and thin, brown skinned with two long braids of black hair, smiled. She wore shorts and a tank top, her nose dusted with freckles.

"I'm Deputy Shane Ellis," he said. "I'm looking for the couple who are leasing a section of the Russell Ranch. I'm wondering if you'd seen them."

Robby removed his leather work gloves and slapped them against his hip, knocking loose a small cloud of dust. "There were two couples over there. They stopped by one day."

"When was this?" Shane asked.

Robby glanced at his wife. "It was this past Tuesday," she said. "I remember because that's my day to deliver eggs and vegetables in town."

"What can you tell me about them?" Shane asked.

"The two men did all the talking," Becca said. "The two women and the little girl didn't have much to say. I asked one of the women if she wanted some chard or onions, and she just shook her head and said, 'No, thank you.' I tried to draw her out a little, asking about where she was from and all, but she wouldn't hardly talk. The other woman, the redhead, just kept her eyes on the older dark-haired man the whole time and ignored me."

Shane took out his notebook and his phone with the photo of Courtney and Ashlyn. "Was this one of the women, and the little girl?" he asked.

The couple put their heads together to view the phone, then both nodded. "That was them," Becca said. "Cute little girl, but she was real shy. Her mother carried her the whole time. I offered to take her to see the chickens, but Mom said no."

"Did they give you their names?" Shane asked.

"The taller, younger man said his name was Troy," Robby said. "The older man was Tom. They didn't introduce the women."

"I thought maybe they were some kind of religious cult or something," Becca said. "But they were dressed normal. The redheaded woman wore a tank top and short shorts, and the other woman and the girl had on pretty sundresses with spaghetti straps. The men had on jeans and polo shirts."

"What did they want?" Shane asked.

"They said they were setting up a ranch on that piece of property next to us and wanted to introduce themselves," Robby said. "But when I tried to find out more, asked where they were from, what they planned to raise on the ranch, and things like that, they changed the subject."

"The way they were looking around, we thought maybe they were checking us out to see what they could steal," Becca said. She hugged her arms over her chest. "I got a bad vibe from the whole bunch. I didn't sleep well for a few nights after their visit, worried they would make trouble."

"What made you think that?" Shane asked.

"They weren't real friendly," Robby said. "And you just get a bad feeling about some people, you know?"

"What did they look like?" Shane asked.

"Troy was fairly tall, with sandy hair," Robby said. "I don't know about his eyes because he kept his sunglasses on the whole time. He was probably in his early thirties, maybe a little younger. The other guy was about forty, a good five inches shorter, and stockier, with dark brown or black hair and an olive complexion. The other woman had long red hair and high cheekbones and long legs."

"She looked like a model," Becca said. "And like she had money. Her clothes were simple, but they looked expensive, and she had gold and diamond jewelry—several rings and earrings and a couple of necklaces."

"Did they say anything about their plans?" Shane asked. "Any details about the ranch or whether or not they planned to live there?"

Robby shook his head. "Troy said he liked our yurt, that it looked more comfortable than the trailer that was on the place they were leasing from Mr. Russell."

"I drive by the entrance to that place a couple of times a week when I go into Eagle Mountain," Becca said. "I haven't seen any sign of anyone over there. I've been meaning to take Mr. Russell some vegetables and eggs and ask him about them, but we've been so busy I haven't had the chance."

"We're putting up an electric fence to keep the bears out of the beehives," Robby said. "We had a big sow snooping around here last week. She got a good jolt from the fence around the pigs and ran out of here."

"I hope that scared her off for good," Becca said. "But we know there are others out there."

Shane looked around, at the greenhouse and live-stock, and the yurt, with its deck dotted with pots of flowers and brightly painted chairs. Behind the yurt he glimpsed a solar array. "You have a nice place here," he said. "Are you off-grid?"

"We are," Robby said. "We have a generator for backup, but mostly we run off solar. And we'd like to put in a wind turbine one day."

Shane took out a card and passed it over. "Let me know if Troy or Tom or the women stop by again."

"Are they wanted for some crime?" Becca asked. "Should we be worried?"

"The blonde woman's family is worried about her," Shane said. "I agreed to contact her if I could, and make sure she was all right."

"She looked okay when we saw her," Becca said. "I mean, she was clean and well-fed and didn't look upset about anything. She was just very quiet." She shrugged. "But some people are quiet. No law against that."

They said goodbye and went back to setting metal posts. Shane walked back to his truck. Was he wasting time, trying to track down Allerton and Courtney? Maybe some people would see it that way, but it would be worth all the hours and effort if he was able to give Lauren some peace of mind. Even hard truth would be better than not knowing.

Chapter Ten

Shane's text to Lauren on Sunday afternoon was cryptic: Meet me my place 6:30 to catch up.

Not exactly an invitation for a romantic rendezvous. She ought to be relieved that he was respecting her request to put some distance between them. Instead, she felt vaguely annoyed. How attracted to her was he if it was so easy for him to switch back to behaving as if their only connection was the case?

As soon as she responded that she'd be there, he replied: I'll get dinner.

Okay. Should she bring wine? Or dessert? Or was that too casual? Too intimate?

She ended up stopping at a bakery and picking up half a dozen cookies. She might have done the same for a meeting at the clinic. She was really overthinking this.

Shane was waiting for her when she arrived, fresh from the shower in jeans and a T-shirt, smelling of soap and aftershave, a combination that made her hyperaware of how masculine and sexy he was. Her gaze fixed on the hint of collarbone visible at the neckline of his shirt, the skin smooth over the bone and looking soft as velvet...

"Lauren? Are you okay?"

She blinked and met his puzzled gaze. "I'm fine." She took a step back and fixed her gaze on the kitchen table, where a bag from a local sandwich shop sat. "What did you get for dinner?"

"Sub sandwiches and chips." He followed her to the table. "There's water or beer, whichever you want."

"Water is fine." She pulled out a chair and sat. She was doing it again—getting obsessed with a man she had just met. Sure, he might profess to be just as interested in her, but those kinds of feelings never lasted. Real relationships took time to nurture and develop, and she didn't have that kind of time to spend in Eagle Mountain. She was here to find Courtney, and she needed to focus on that mission, not Shane.

"What have you found out about Courtney?" she asked when he returned to the table with two glasses of water.

"I stopped by the Russell Ranch before work yesterday." He settled into the chair across from her. "Mr. Russell hadn't seen her, or Trey. But he did receive a check for ten thousand dollars two days ago—the deadline for making the next lease payment. So I think we know how the money Courtney asked for was used."

A weight settled in Lauren's stomach. "I'm relieved Ashlyn isn't really sick, though I guess I already knew that. But it hurts to know Courtney lied. That isn't like her at all."

"Maybe you have an idealized version of your sister-in-law," he said. "It's not wrong to want to think the best of people, and she probably only showed you her best side. But that doesn't mean this other side of her hasn't been there all along."

"Maybe." Lauren popped a potato chip into her mouth and crunched it. Shane was a cop, and his job probably forced him to be cynical about people's intentions. But she knew Courtney wasn't dishonest. "I think Trey Allerton forced her to tell those lies," she said. "He either played on her sympathy and made her believe he was desperate and had to have her help, or worse, he bullied her or threatened her to make her do what he wanted." She met Shane's gaze, wanting him to see how concerned she was. "We won't know until we find her, and if he's threatening her, we really need to find her soon."

He nodded and picked up his sandwich. "I visited the neighbors who live on the other side of the property Allerton leased from Samuel Russell," he said. "A young couple who are homesteading the property, Becca and Robby Olsen. They live in a yurt, and they said Allerton, Courtney, Ashlyn and another couple stopped by there last Tuesday."

Lauren choked on the bite of sandwich she was chewing. As she coughed, Shane hurried around to pound her back. She took a swig of water and waited for the spasm to calm, then said, "Are they living at the ranch? Did you check there?"

"I stopped by there on the way out, but there's still no sign of them in that old trailer, or anywhere else that I could see." He returned to his chair. "The other couple with Allerton and Courtney sound like the ones Mr. Russell described—a dark-haired, stocky man and a tall redhead. They identified Courtney and Ashlyn from your photo. Becca said the redheaded woman with them had expensive clothing and jewelry and looked like a model."

"That sounds like Talia Larrivee," Lauren said. "That's how I would describe her."

Shane froze in the act of raising his sandwich to his lips. "I hadn't thought of that," he said. "And the man—forties, stocky, with dark hair and olive skin— that sounds like the man Talia was with at ball practice the other day. And she called him Tom. That's the name Allerton's partner was using. I feel like an idiot for not making the connection before."

"You've seen this man?" Lauren leaned toward him. "Do you think Trey was with him then? Was he with another man?"

"He was with Talia," Shane said. "I didn't see him talking to or interacting with anyone else."

"But you were focused on playing baseball," she said. "Maybe Trey, and Courtney, too, were there and you didn't notice." She stood. "We need to talk to other people who were at that practice. Maybe someone noticed them. They can at least tell us if Courtney and Ashlyn are okay."

"They weren't there," Shane said. "And as of last Tuesday, at least, Courtney and Ashlyn were fine. Becca Olsen described them as clean, well-fed and quiet."

"I imagine prisoners get described that way sometimes." She sat back down. She hated this frustration, of knowing something was wrong but being unable to persuade anyone else of her suspicions. "How did Trey and Courtney end up with Talia and this Tom fellow?" she asked.

"I'm pretty sure Talia's father has a house in Denver. Maybe Courtney and Talia met there. They're close to the same age."

"And have nothing in common," Lauren said. "Courtney is a mom and a homebody. And she doesn't care about fancy clothes or jewelry."

"Opposites attract in friendship as well as romance," he said. "Or maybe Allerton and Tom know each other and Allerton brought him in because he needed a partner for his youth ranch."

"He told Courtney he and Mike planned to partner to build the ranch," Lauren said. "He wanted her to be part of the project in Mike's place. I really think that's the only reason she agreed to the plan—because she thought it was what Mike wanted."

He was giving her that look again—part sympathy and part skepticism. "I know you think I'm only seeing what I want to see," she said. "But Courtney is not in love with Trey. Maybe she's physically attracted to him, and I get that she might enjoy having him pay attention to her. But I saw the way she looked at my brother, before and after they were married, and she never looked at Allerton that way. Not even close."

"Even if she isn't in love with him, she may have agreed to partner with him in the ranch because she wanted to help young people," Shane said. "Or she thought it would give her purpose in life, or allow her to make a fresh start or any of a dozen other legitimate reasons."

"But we'll need to talk to her to find that out," Lauren said. She crunched another chip. "So what do we do next?"

"I need to see what else I can find out about Tom," he said. "I'll stop by Russell Ranch and see if I can talk to Mr. Russell again."

"What can I do?" she asked.

"Get in touch with some of Courtney's other friends. Ask if they ever heard her mention Talia or Tom. And talk to your friend at the law office. Tell her to call you if Courtney requests more money from her trust."

"Should I tell her we suspect Courtney is lying about what the money is being used for?"

"I'll leave that up to you."

It felt like a betrayal, to accuse Courtney of lying that way. What she had done might even be illegal. "I don't think I'll say any more than I have to right now," she said. One day—she hoped soon—Courtney would want to come home and settle into her old life again. Lauren wanted to make that transition as smooth as possible.

"There's nothing else we can do tonight," he said. "Let's just enjoy our meal and talk about something else."

"All right. Tell me about this Independence Day celebration. I've seen posters around town. Besides the baseball game between the sheriff's department and the fire department, what else happens? Fireworks?"

He nodded and finished chewing. "There's a big fireworks show after dark, against the backdrop of Dakota Ridge. A parade in the morning."

"A parade? Like, with floats and marching bands?"

"One band, from the high school, and the floats are mostly just pickup trucks towing flatbed trailers with people on the back throwing out candy. But there are people on horseback and kids on bikes and people waving flags. It's one of those small-town things."

"It sounds charming," she said. "I'll be sure not to miss it."

"The history museum hands out lemonade and dresses in old-timey outfits in front of the museum," he said. "And the Elks sell barbecue in the park. The 4-H kids set up a carnival with face painting and little games and a dunking booth."

"When is the baseball game?" she asked. "And where is it?"

"The only field in town is at the high school," he said. "The game is at three o'clock on Sunday. They used to play in old-timey gray flannel uniforms and flat caps, but the uniforms wore out after a few years, and they were so hot and uncomfortable that guys refused to play if they couldn't wear jeans and T-shirts, so the committee gave in."

"Do a lot of people attend?" she asked.

"Seems like," he said. "Adelaide tells me they're selling tickets as fast as they can print them. She's looking for volunteers to sell concessions at the game. Sign up and you'll get in free."

"Maybe I'll do that." It would probably be better than watching by herself in the stands.

His phone rang, dancing across the tabletop as it vibrated. He picked it up and frowned at the screen. "It's the sheriff," he said.

She went to refill their water glasses while he answered the call. When she returned, he was holding the phone, looking disturbed. "What did the sheriff want?" she asked.

"He's asking everyone to report for duty," he said. "Evan Larrivee called and said Talia called him and said she was scared and in trouble. Now he doesn't know where she is."

Chapter Eleven

Sheriff Travis Walker assembled his force in the conference room at headquarters Sunday evening, his usual
solemn expression betraying nothing. "Evan Larrivee
called my personal number a little after six this evening to report that he had a very concerning phone call
from his daughter, Talia. She told him she was afraid
and begged him to come get her, but before she could
say where she was, the connection broke off. He hasn't
been able to reach her since."

"He called your personal number?" Gage asked.
"Not Dispatch?"

"He didn't want to raise an alarm," Travis said. "But
after talking to him, I think there might be reason for
concern."

Several of the deputies exchanged looks. "What's
happened?" Jamie Douglas, the force's only female deputy, asked.

"The last time Evan saw Talia was two days ago,"
Travis said. "She said she was going on a trip into the
mountains with friends, but when Evan asked her who
these friends were, her answer was 'You wouldn't know

them.' He didn't hear anything from her until her frantic phone call this evening. He said she sounded really scared, but before he could find out more, the call ended. He couldn't say whether the call dropped, or someone took the phone from her."

"Where were Talia and these friends headed?" Dwight asked.

"She wouldn't say," Travis said. "Evan says that's unusual. He says Talia is always trying to shock him with stories about her wild adventures and rarely withholds information, though she's been known to embellish. He got the sense she was hiding something, and that worried him."

"She was at ball practice Friday evening," Gage said. "With a man I'd never seen before."

"Adelaide said she overheard Talia call the guy Tom," Shane said. "And I'm pretty sure the two of them were up at Robby and Becca Olsen's place, out by Samuel Russell's ranch, last Wednesday, with Courtney Baker and Trey Allerton."

Every eye in the room focused on him. "Courtney Baker is Lauren Baker's sister-in-law," Travis said. "Lauren came to Eagle Mountain from Denver to look for her and asked for our help, but we couldn't find any evidence of foul play, or that Courtney left with Allerton of anything but her own accord."

"In my spare time, I've been helping Lauren trace Courtney's footsteps," Shane explained. "Yesterday morning, I talked to the Olsens, and they told me about seeing Allerton and Courtney on Tuesday with a man called Tom and a red-haired woman in expensive clothes who looked like a model."

"That sounds like Talia," Gage said.

"I thought so, too," Shane said. Especially after Lauren had pointed it out to him.

"Talia has had a lot of different male friends," Dwight said. "Is there any reason to be particularly concerned about this one?"

"Evan said when he asked her why she wouldn't tell him the names of the people she was with, she said, 'My new boyfriend wouldn't like it.' After he received that last call from her, he drove around town and found her car in the high school lot, and someone told him it's been there since Friday afternoon."

"Could this be Talia playing a trick on her dad?" Jamie asked. "Trying to get attention?"

"He says no, that he's convinced she was truly terrified when she contacted him," Travis said. "I want everyone to keep an eye out for her. Talk to people who might have seen her and follow up on any leads. If she's just rebelling against her father's authority with friends he wouldn't approve of, we'll find that out soon enough. But if she's in real trouble, we want to be in the best position to help her." He turned to Shane. "What were Courtney and her friends doing up by the Olsens?"

"Trey Allerton leased a section of the Russell Ranch that borders the Olsens' property," Shane said. "He says he wants to turn it into a retreat for troubled youth. He talked Courtney Baker into contributing money to the project, and he's introduced this Tom guy as his business partner."

"Any reason to suspect the retreat is a cover for something else?" Gage asked.

Shane shook his head. "There's no sign of any work being done on the property they leased, but maybe they're waiting for more funding or plans or something. The only thing suspicious is that Courtney Baker lied to get the money for the second lease payment. She told the lawyers who manage her trust fund that she needed ten thousand dollars to pay her daughter's medical bills. That's the exact amount of the payment Allerton made to Russell the day after Courtney withdrew the money."

"Did you talk to Sam Russell about all of this?" Travis asked.

"I did. He said Tom didn't say much—Allerton did all the talking. But he said Tom had prison tattoos. He recognized them because he's had ex-cons work for him on the ranch."

"That surprises me a little," Gage said. "Not that Tom has prison ink, but that Russell hires ex-cons."

"He said he believes in giving people a second chance."

"Let's see if we can get a last name for Tom and find out if he has a criminal record," Travis said. "Shane, you come with me to talk to Larrivee. Let's see what he knows about Tom, and Talia's other new friends."

Evan Larrivee had a shaved head, a neatly trimmed goatee showing the first signs of gray and the sagging features of a man who has not slept well. "I know Talia can be very high-spirited," he said when Travis and

Shane stopped by his home to interview him. "She's done things before that worried me, but this feels different."

"You said before that your daughter is twenty-two," Travis said. "Has she gone off like this before?"

"I know what you're thinking," Larrivee said. "She's an adult. She doesn't have to report to me. But as long as she lives under my roof and I support her, she does." He visibly reined in his emotions. "That may sound antagonistic, and I don't mean it to. Talia and I have a good relationship. When she called me to ask for help, it's because she knew I would drop everything to get to her. If only I knew where she was." His voice broke and he looked away.

"What friends does she go off with?" Travis asked.

Larrivee pulled himself together. "Girlfriends, mostly," he said. "She has two or three she pals around with. But I already talked to them and they haven't heard from her, either."

"We'll need their names so we can talk to them," Travis said.

"Fine, but they don't know anything. You need to find the people she's with."

"Who is that?" Shane asked.

"If I knew that, I wouldn't have bothered you people," Larrivee said.

"But you believe Talia isn't alone?" Travis asked. "That she is with other people? What can you tell us about them?"

Larrivee shook his head. "I never met them. She mentioned a new boyfriend but wouldn't tell me his name. I finally got one of her friends to admit that there was a man, and she thinks his name is Tom, but she swore that's all she knew."

Travis pulled out his phone. "What's the friend's name?" he asked.

"Anne-Marie Winstead Jones," Larrivee said. "She said she saw Talia with the man once and he looked kind of rough."

"Rough how?" Shane asked.

Larrivee shrugged. "Just…rough. And older. Late thirties or early forties, she said." He pressed his lips together in a thin line.

"Has your daughter dated older men before?" Shane asked.

"No. And from what Anne-Marie told me, this guy was no looker. Talia can have her pick of men, but she's young. She likes to have fun. Which is another reason I don't understand her association with this guy. He's not her usual type."

"What is her type?" Travis asked.

"You know—young, like her. With enough money to show her a good time. And good-looking. She dates athletes—rock climbers, skiers, that kind of thing. She likes dare-devils and risk takers, but this guy sounded different."

"Is it possible this Tom targeted your daughter?" Shane asked. "Maybe he charmed her because he's interested in her money."

"My daughter is used to dealing with fortune hunters," Larrivee said. "I taught her about them from the time she was a young teen. She's dated a lot of men, but if they show a hint of being interested in her money, she drops them like that." He snapped his fingers.

"You mentioned you believed your daughter left with more than one person," Travis said. "Who are the other people involved?"

"I don't know. Before she left, she said she was going off for a few days with friends. When I asked her who these friends were, she said she couldn't tell me, that her new boyfriend wouldn't like it. That set off all kinds of alarm bells, I tell you. But when I tried to question her further, she told me she'd call me later, and she hung up. Since then, all my calls go straight to voice mail and she doesn't respond to my texts, either." Some of the authority went out of his voice. "I'm really worried."

Travis made a few notes on his phone, then tucked it away. "We'd like to see your daughter's room," he said.

"This way." Larrivee led the way up a curving flight of stairs. "I already searched it. I didn't find anything but a little pot and some cigarettes. I don't approve of either and Talia knows it, which was probably why they were hidden, but they're not illegal here, so there's not too much I can do about them except order her not to use them in my presence."

Talia Larrivee's room—or rather, a suite of rooms—occupied a large portion of the second floor, with a bedroom, large sitting room, smaller dressing room and wardrobe, and an expansive bathroom. "Does she keep a datebook or diary?" Travis asked.

Larrivee snorted. "That's all on her phone, and she has that with her. Though the tracking software has been turned off."

At Shane's startled look, Larrivee laughed. "I designed that software, Deputy. Of course I had it on my daughter's phone. But someone switched it off or removed it outright."

"Would Talia know how to do that?" Travis asked.

"She would," he said. "She might come across as an airhead, but my daughter is very smart."

"We'd like to have a look around, if you don't mind," Travis said.

"Don't you need a warrant for that?" Larrivee asked.

"I can get one, if that would make you feel better," Travis said, his expression deadpan, as usual.

"Nothing is going to make me feel better except finding my little girl," Larrivee said. He stepped back. "Go ahead. I've already seen everything in here, anyway." He moved to the door. "I'll be downstairs if you need me."

When he was gone, Travis pulled on a pair of gloves and moved to the desk. "What do you think?" he asked Shane.

Shane, who was slipping on his own gloves, said, "A twenty-two-year-old whose father still lays down the law and controls the purse strings, and who doesn't think twice about going through her personal belongings—I think most people would rebel against that at some point."

"So she could just be asserting her independence by going away for a few days with a man she knows Daddy won't approve of." Travis began thumbing through the books on the bedside table. "That doesn't explain the frantic phone call. And she seems to have crossed paths with another woman who left suddenly with a man her relatives—or one relative, at least—didn't like, who is also refusing to return calls." He shook his head. "I don't like coincidences like that."

"We don't know that any of them are breaking any laws," Shane said. He swept his hand under the edge of a bookshelf, searching for anything that might be taped under there.

"No, but they might be on the edge of illegal," Travis said. "I'd like to know for sure."

"The lease of the land from Russell is legitimate," Shane said. "Though there's no sign of any work being done on the place. Could the youth ranch idea be a cover for something else?"

"You say Courtney Baker has money?"

"Several million, according to Lauren," Shane said. "But most of it is tied up in a trust."

"Maybe Allerton thinks he can get control of the trust." Travis opened the top drawer of the dresser.

"Where does Tom come in?" Shane asked. "According to Russell, he didn't have much to say, but Allerton introduced him as his partner."

"Don't know," Travis said. He pulled out the drawer and lifted it up to peer under it. "There's something here."

Shane joined him, and Travis handed him the drawer, then took out his phone and photographed the bottom of it. He pocketed the phone once more and retrieved his pocketknife, which he used to pry off a small brown envelope that was taped to the underside of the dresser drawer. He laid it on the top of the dresser and, with gloved fingers, teased open the flap.

The picture inside was a woman, naked except for a lacy pink bra, her hands tied in front of her with rope, and more rope wound around and around her, a black cloth gag in her mouth. She lay on a bed, dark hair in a tangle on the pillow around her, her skin very white against dark sheets. She stared at the camera, eyes wide with terror.

"That isn't Courtney Baker or Talia Larrivee," Shane said.

"No." Travis slid the photo back into the envelope. "But we need to find out who this is. Larrivee may be right—his daughter may be involved in something dangerous."

Monday morning, Lauren inched her car along the rough gravel road that wound up the mountain, past the Russell Ranch. Had she missed the turnoff to the little trailer she and Shane had visited? It had seemed so easy to get to when she was with him, but today everything looked different.

She hadn't told Shane she planned to drive out here. If Courtney and Trey were leasing this place, then she had a right to visit, didn't she? Maybe she'd get lucky and Courtney would be here. Lauren would try to persuade her to come back to town with her. Maybe she would invite Courtney and Ashlyn to have lunch, and once she had them alone, she'd persuade her sister-in-law to return to Denver with her. At the very least, she could hear from Courtney herself what was really going on.

If Courtney and Trey weren't at the trailer or nearby, Lauren would do a more thorough search and hope to find evidence of where they might be. If she found anything, she'd share the information with Shane, but if she didn't, there was no need for him to know she had even been here.

The Prius rattled across the cattle guard, and she spotted the driveway to the right and turned in. Up a small rise and the trailer rose into view, ugly and abandoned. No vehicle waited in the driveway, and the windows stared vacantly at the barren yard. Lauren parked her car in the shade of a leaning juniper and got out, the echo of the car door slamming making her flinch. If Courtney and Allerton were anywhere within hearing distance, they would know someone had stopped by. She hoped they would come to find out who.

Every nerve taut, she crossed to the steps and mounted them. The door swung open easily, and she stepped inside. At first glance, it seemed nothing had changed since she had been here with Shane. Trash still littered the mud-colored carpet, and the broken chair still leaned to one side in the corner. Lauren wrinkled her nose in disgust. If Courtney really was planning to live here with Trey and Ashlyn, she would have started cleaning right away. She would have thrown out every stick of furniture in the place and filled the rooms with simple, but tasteful, items she chose. The new furnishings wouldn't necessarily be expensive, but they would be comfortable, sturdy and pleasing to the eye. Courtney wasn't flashy or extravagant, but she had a knack for making a place into a home. Mike had always said that if he decided on a career in the military, Courtney would be able to make anywhere he was stationed warm and comfortable.

Lauren moved toward the bedroom and bathroom where she had found Ashlyn's doll when she had been here before. The first time she had met Courtney, she had been impressed by the young woman's combination of striking beauty and humble sweetness. And by how utterly besotted Mike was with his new girlfriend. Mike was handsome and outgoing and had dated many women, most of them very nice. But Lauren knew something was different between him and Courtney from that very first meeting. Mike couldn't take his eyes off Courtney, and when he spoke about her, his voice took on a tone of mingled pride and reverence.

"I think she's the woman I want to spend the rest of my life with," he had confided to Lauren a few weeks later. "I've never met anyone like her, and I think she feels the same about me."

Indeed, Courtney had been every bit as devoted to Mike. Had that devotion, even after Mike's death, colored her judgment? "Did Mike ever mention anything to you about Trey Allerton and this youth ranch?" Lauren had asked the last time the two women had spoken, after Courtney had announced that she had decided to be a part of Allerton's plans.

"No," Courtney admitted.

"Don't you think if this project was as dear to his heart as Allerton is trying to get you to believe, Mike would have said something to you?" Lauren asked. "He didn't hide things from you, did he?"

"Not that I know of, but maybe he was saving this to tell me when he came home. You know how generous Mike was, and how much he loved children. This is exactly the kind of project he'd be excited about."

Courtney was right. Mike would have loved the idea of a ranch in the mountains where kids could come to relax and get away from their problems, and maybe learn new coping skills or discover new strengths. But Lauren couldn't believe her brother had trusted someone like Trey Allerton. "I'm worried about you trusting too much in Trey," she told Courtney. "I think he's only interested in your money."

"The money isn't even mine," Courtney said. "It was Mike's money, and I want to do something with it to make him proud. I know you think I'm naive about people because I choose to believe the best in them, but I'm not stupid."

Lauren heard the hurt behind the words. "I know you're not stupid," she said, her voice gentle.

Courtney smiled and squeezed Lauren's hand. "Thank you for that. But sometimes your feelings show so clearly in your eyes. I'm going to be all right, you'll see. I don't even care if this wasn't Mike's dream. I know it's something he would approve of, so I'm going to do my best to make it happen."

"But how are you making it happen?" Lauren asked out loud. She looked around the deserted bedroom. "By lying to get money? By refusing to return calls and texts from the people who love you?"

A sound behind her made her turn around. A wiry man in dirty jeans and a faded plaid shirt stood in the doorway to the bedroom. "Who are you?" he demanded. Then he reached behind him and drew a pistol from a holster at his back and aimed the gun at her. "Around here, we shoot trespassers."

Chapter Twelve

Lauren froze, heart hammering, gaze locked on the gun. "What are you doing?" she asked, angry at the tremor in her voice but unable to control it.

"I asked you first. What are you doing here?" The rangy man jabbed the gun in her direction.

She flinched. "I'm looking for my sister-in-law, Courtney."

"What makes you think she's here? Nobody's here. You're trespassing on private property."

Lauren kept her gaze on the gun and stood up straighter, mustering her courage. "You're the one who's trespassing. My sister and her...her business partner leased this property from Mr. Russell."

"So you know about that, do you?"

"Who are you, and what are you doing here?"

"My name's King—Von King. Mr. Allen hired me to do some work on the place and to keep an eye on it while he's away."

Mr. Allen. He must mean Trey Allerton. "Where is he?" she asked. "I need to talk to him." She had nothing to say to Allerton, but she desperately wanted to speak to Courtney.

King shoved the pistol back in its holster. "It's above my pay grade to keep track of his comings and goings. And if you're such good friends with him, why don't you know?"

"I never said I was friends with him. But I'm good friends with Courtney."

"Who's Courtney?"

"She's the woman who's traveling with Allerton. Short, blonde, with blue eyes. She has a little girl."

The wicked glint in King's eyes made her shrink back. "So that's her name," he said.

"You've seen her?"

He leered. "A man's not likely to forget a woman who looks like that."

"I need to speak with her. Tell me Allerton's number and I'll call him."

"You keep calling him Allerton, but he told me his name is Allen."

She said nothing, merely glared at him.

King grinned, revealing gaps where half a dozen teeth were missing. "That's okay," he said. "My real name isn't King, either."

He turned away, his laughter trailing him all the way to his truck. He slammed the door, the engine roared to life and he raced away, kicking up a rooster tail of dust. Lauren leaned against the bedroom wall and stared out the window after him. Inside, she was shaking, with anger and with fear.

SHANE COULDN'T ERASE the image of that terrified bound woman from his memory, even long after he had left the sheriff's department and headed out to question Robby and Becca Olsen again. The image itself was disturbing enough, but why had Talia had it at all? And why had she concealed it under that dresser drawer? When they had shown the photo to Evan Larrivee, he had recoiled, visibly shaken. "I've never seen that before," he said. "It's not of anyone we know, I'm sure. Why would Talia have that?"

By the time Travis and Shane had left the Larrivee home Sunday evening, Evan was already rationalizing the discovery of the picture. "It could have been taped under that drawer for years," he said. "I'm sure it has nothing to do with Talia."

Shane was sure the picture had not been there long. The tape holding it looked fresh, and the image itself wasn't yellowed or faded with age.

He passed the entrance to the Russell Ranch. He needed to talk to Russell again, but he wanted to interview the Olsens again first. They had seen Tom and company most recently. He tried to focus on the interview ahead. He needed the Olsens to go over every detail of their visit with Tom, Courtney, Trey and a woman he believed was Talia. He had a good photo of Talia to show them, and he hoped they would remember something one of the four had said to indicate where they might be staying.

He rounded a curve and braked hard as a car raced toward him, the driver straddling the center of the narrow gravel road, driving much too fast. He bumped the siren so that it let out a single whoop as a warning, and the car skidded to the side and came to a stop on the shoulder. He pulled alongside it and was startled to see Lauren, fumbling with her seat belt.

By the time he unfastened his own seat belt and opened the car door, she was standing alongside him. "Thank God I ran into you," she said. The words came out in a rush and she was breathless.

He slid out of the vehicle and took her by the shoulders. "What's wrong?" he asked. "What's happened?"

She glanced over her shoulder, then relaxed a little, as if she'd been worried someone was following her. "Did another car pass you, headed out?" she asked. "Or maybe a truck? Yes, I'm sure it was a truck."

"Yours is the first vehicle I've met," he said. "Come on." He led her around to the passenger side of the cruiser. "Get in and tell me what this is about."

She slid into the seat, and he retrieved a bottle of water from a cooler in the rear of the cruiser, then returned to the driver's seat and handed it to her. She didn't open it but held it in both hands and turned toward him. "I drove out to the place Trey is leasing from Samuel Russell," she said. "I wanted to look at the trailer again and see if I could find any indication that Courtney had been there recently. Really, I was hoping she and Trey would be there and I could talk to them."

"Lauren—" he began, but she cut him off.

"If you're going to tell me I shouldn't have gone out there alone, don't waste your breath. I couldn't sit in that rental one more minute without doing something and I'm fine."

She hadn't been fine when she first flagged him down, but he decided he'd be better off keeping quiet and letting her talk. He merely nodded to indicate she should keep going.

"The trailer was open, so I went inside. Honestly, the place is a pit. I can't see Courtney in it—she's always kept such a nice house, and she'd be miserable so far from town, with no close neighbors."

"We don't know that they planned to live there," he said.

"You're right." She sighed. "And I didn't see any sign that anyone had been there since you and I checked it out on Wednesday. I was ready to leave when the man came in behind me and threatened me with a gun."

Anger and shock climbed up Shane's spine. "Are you okay? Who was this guy?"

"I'm fine." She knotted her hands together. "He scared me, but after I talked to him a bit, he put the gun away. He said his name was Von King, and that Trey Allerton—only he called him Troy Allen—had hired him to look after the place he was leasing from Russell. And then, before he left, he said his name wasn't really Von King."

"What did he look like?" Shane took out his phone and began making notes.

"He was medium height, thin and wiry, with thinning dirty-blond hair."

"How old?" Shane asked.

"I'm not sure. Forties? Maybe older, maybe younger. He needed a shave and his beard had some gray in it, but he looked like a man who spent a lot of time out of doors and had lived a hard life—leathery skin with a lot of wrinkles."

"What did he say to you?"

"He knew Courtney." She frowned. "He made some comment about how pretty she was. I tried to get him to tell me how to get in touch with her or with Trey, but he wouldn't answer. He just put the gun away and left. I did, too. I was worried he might follow me, but I don't know where he went." She opened the bottle of water and took a long drink, then settled back in the seat. "What are you doing out here?"

"I was on my way to speak to the Olsens," he said.

"Let me go with you," she said. "I want to know if they remember anything else about Courtney and Ashlyn."

He wanted to tell her to go back to her rental and wait for him, but her description of her encounter with Von King disturbed him, and he didn't think it would be a bad idea to keep her close for a little while longer. "All right," he said. "Do you want to follow me in your car, or ride in the cruiser?"

"My car should be all right parked here, shouldn't it?" She smiled. "I'll feel better riding with you."

The thought cheered him, though she was probably only saying that because he was a cop. They passed no other vehicles on the drive to the Olsens' and pulled up to the yurt a few moments later. "Hello!" Shane called as he climbed out of the cruiser.

"I don't see anyone around," Lauren said. Somewhere to their left, a chicken squawked, but otherwise, all was silent.

"Maybe they're in the house," Shane said. He strode to the front door and knocked.

No one answered. "What now?" Lauren asked when he returned to the cruiser.

"Let's see if we can find another neighbor," he said. "Maybe Allerton and company visited them, too."

He turned left out of the Olsens' driveway and continued on the same road, which became much rougher after they passed the fence marking the end of the Olsens' property. The grade grew steeper, climbing into the mountains near the tree line. They passed the weathered wooden frame and rusting cable of an old mine tram, and a pile of rubble that might have once been a cabin. "I can't imagine living in such rugged country," Lauren said. "It's beautiful this time of year, but I'm imagining how it must look in winter."

"There's a lot of snow at this elevation," he said. "And I'm pretty sure the county doesn't plow past Russell's driveway."

"How do people get around?"

"Snowmobile, or they plow for themselves. It takes an independent personality to live up here year round. But then, that's the type who end up here. They're willing to trade the inconveniences for cheaper land and few regulations."

He slowed as he neared a hand-painted sign at the end of a faint track leading across rocky ground. Full Moon Mine. No Trespassing. Owner Is Armed.

"Not exactly welcoming," Lauren said.

"No, but someone with an attitude like that is likely to remember anyone who stopped by." Shane swung the cruiser into the drive. He drove slowly for half a mile over increasingly rough ground, passing two more

No Trespassing signs, one of which featured a drawing of a skull.

At the top of the hill, Shane stopped the cruiser in front of a shack made of split logs set on end, a rusting metal roof sloping steeply over a door made from a larger slab of wood. Shane maneuvered the cruiser so that it faced back the way they had come, and he left the engine running. "Stay here until I've checked this out," he said.

"You're making me nervous," she said, aware of the tension radiating from him.

"I'm just being cautious." As he exited the cruiser, the door of the shack swung open and a man dressed in canvas pants and a dirty gray shirt stepped out, a long gun cradled in his arms.

"You're trespassing," he said in a loud, clear voice. "You've got thirty seconds to get back in that vehicle and leave."

"Are you Martin Kramer?" Shane asked. He sounded relaxed, but his spine had stiffened, and one hand hovered over the pistol at his side.

"Who wants to know?"

"Deputy Sheriff Shane Ellis. I need you to put the gun down, sir."

"What are you going to do if I don't? Shoot me?"

"Please, put the gun away, sir," Shane said. "I'm looking for some people who may have stopped by here."

The wrinkles running across Kramer's face like gullies deepened, but he set the gun aside, leaning it against the wall of the shack. "I get all kinds of people come through here," he said. "You ought to do your job and arrest them for trespassing."

"Are you Martin Kramer?" Shane asked again. "I like to know who I'm talking to."

"I'm him," Kramer said. "What has this bunch you're looking for done?"

"I just need to talk to them," Shane said. "Have you had any visitors in the last couple of weeks? Two men, maybe with two women. They may also have had a little girl."

"Who's that in the car with you?" Kramer jerked his head toward Lauren. "Tell her to come out where I can see her."

"Come on out, Lauren," Shane said, his gaze still fixed on Kramer.

Lauren got out of the cruiser. "Hello," she said, walking around to stand near Shane. "I'm Lauren. One of the women we're looking for is my brother's widow. The little girl is my niece. I've been really worried about them."

"Is she the blonde or the redhead?" Kramer asked.

Lauren's heart lurched. "You've seen them? They were here?"

Kramer looked skyward. "What is it with you people who can't answer a direct question?"

"Courtney is blonde," Lauren said. She glanced at Shane. He hadn't moved, gaze still locked on Kramer, right hand near the pistol. This is what it's like being a deputy, she thought. Always alert for trouble.

"When were they here?" Shane asked.

"Three or four days ago. Two men—a big young guy who did all the talking, a shorter, darker man and two good-looking women and a little girl. I told them to clear on out, but the big one was like you—he didn't listen. He asked a lot of nosy questions about my operation—stuff that was none of his business. I had to fire a warning shot to get him to shut up and leave."

"Your operation?" Shane asked.

"My gold mine. I'm not some crazy hermit who thought it would be fun to live in a shack on a mountain. I work for a living. But it's not enough that I have to break my back in the mine—I've got to contend with trespassers and thieves?"

"Who's been stealing from you and what have they stolen?" Shane asked.

"That big guy with all his questions about the mine was a claim jumper or my name is Shirley Temple," Kramer said. "People think that kind of thing died out with the Old West, but greed never goes extinct."

"How would they steal your claim?" Lauren asked. "Did they threaten you?"

"They knew better than that," he said. "I had a gun and they didn't, or at least they didn't have one out where I could see it. But nowadays thieves don't need weapons to take what isn't theirs. They find out all about you and the claim, then they go on the computer and file papers and such, and the next thing you know, they've robbed you blind. I've known it to happen to other folks, but by gum, I won't let them do it to me."

"Did the man tell you his name?" Shane asked.

"He did not. He just launched right in with a spiel about how they were looking to buy land in the area and did I know of any for sale, and did I think any of these old mining claims around here were worth investing in and was I having much success on my own claim? The more he talked, the madder I got. And while he was going on and on, the other fellow was looking around at everything like he was taking inventory. A bunch of thieves for sure, ready to rob me blind."

Lauren couldn't see anything on the property worth taking, but that was beside the point. "What did the two women do?" she asked.

"The redhead hovered near the dark-haired guy, looking nervous. The blonde was fussing with the little girl, who was whining about wanting to go home. That little girl had more sense than the rest of them."

"This was on Thursday or Friday?" Shane asked.

"About that. I didn't mark it on the calendar."

"Did the man say where they had come from, or where they were headed next?" Shane asked.

"I didn't care enough to pay attention if they did," Kramer said. "I wanted them gone. The big guy didn't shut up until I fired my shotgun in the air."

"What happened then?" Lauren asked, trying to imagine the scene.

"The redhead screamed and latched on to the dark-haired man. The little girl started crying and the blonde picked her up, and the big guy swore at me. But he turned around and headed back to his car and the others followed him."

"What was he driving?" Shane asked.

"A black SUV. One of the big ones. New looking, with Colorado plates. I didn't get the number."

"Have you seen or heard from them since?" Shane asked.

"No. And I've been watching for them to come back. If they go near the mine, they'll be sorry."

"What do you mean by that?" Shane asked.

Kramer's scowl deepened. "Never you mind. If you find that bunch, I want to charge them with trespassing."

"They could charge you with threatening them with a weapon," Shane said.

"A man's got a right to protect his property. Now I've said all I've got to say." He folded his arms. "You can leave now."

"All right." Shane slipped a card from his shirt pocket. "If you see these people again, give me a call." He extended the card to Kramer.

"Don't have a telephone," Kramer said. "No service up here."

"I'll leave this, anyway." Shane laid the card atop a nearby boulder. He waited for Lauren to get into the cruiser before he eased into the driver's seat, waiting until the last minute to turn his back on Kramer.

Lauren looked over her shoulder as they started back down the rough road. Kramer was cradling the shotgun again. She couldn't see his face, but she imagined him scowling.

Shane let out a long breath. "That could have gone badly," he said.

"The gun frightened me," she said.

"He meant it to. But I think Trey and the rest of them frightened him."

The observation surprised her. "Why do you say that?"

"He's one older man, up here all alone," Shane said. "There was fear behind his bluster, I'm sure of it."

"Do you think Trey was interested in stealing the mine?"

"You know him better than I do," Shane said. "What do you think?"

She pondered the question for the next few minutes, as Shane navigated the last half mile of the rough track. "I think he needs money," she said. "I still believe that's why he focused on Courtney. Maybe he saw another opportunity with the gold mine, though that doesn't really sound like a good source for quick cash."

"I'm trying to figure out Tom's role in all of this," Shane said. He shifted into a lower gear as they started down a steep slope.

"Trey introduced him to Mr. Russell as his partner," she said. "So maybe he supplied some of the money Trey needs."

"Why does Allerton need money?"

"For the youth ranch?" Though she hadn't believed he was serious about that project—it was just a way to play on Courtney's sympathies. "Do you think he might be involved in some kind of criminal activity?" she asked.

"I don't know," he said. "But I can't say he's acting like someone with nothing to hide."

"Courtney wouldn't have anything to do with him if she believed he was breaking the law," she said. "Not voluntarily." That was what worried her most—her sister-in-law and niece held hostage somehow by a man Lauren had never trusted.

They fell silent as they headed back down the mountain. As they passed the Olsens' yurt, the door opened and Becca Olsen ran toward them, waving her arms and shouting for them to stop.

Shane braked sharply and skidded to a stop. He and Lauren hurried out. "What's wrong?" Shane asked.

Becca's face was pale, her eyes red rimmed, as if she had been crying. "We were just going to call you," she said. "The most awful thing has happened."

Robby joined them and put an arm around his wife's shoulders. He was pale, too, his expression grim. "Becca and I were hiking in the wilderness area at the end of this road," he said, pointing back the way Shane and Lauren has just traveled. "The Sanford Mine trail. We were exploring some of the old mine ruins." He swallowed, Adam's apple convulsing. "We found a body. A woman. And I don't think she'd been dead long."

Chapter Thirteen

Shane called in for backup, then left Lauren with Becca while he and Robby drove to the end of the road. They parked at the trailhead for the Sanford Mine trail, then hiked another two miles to the mining ruins.

"The body is in there," Robby said, indicating a mostly intact cabin. Though the windows and door were missing, the rest of the structure looked sound. "In the back corner. We thought it was a pile of old clothes at first." He put a hand to his mouth.

Shane patted his shoulder. "You stay out here while I have a look." He approached the cabin, forcing aside emotion, focusing on the job. Nothing about the place looked disturbed. Nothing marred the slab of rock that served as a doorstep. Fallen leaves and the remains of a pack rat nest made of dried grasses and twigs littered the eight-by-eight room. He unclipped a flashlight from his belt and directed the beam into the corner.

The woman lay curled on her side, red hair obscuring her face, one arm stretched out in front of her. When he moved closer, he could see the red-black blood staining the back of her head. Carefully, he bent and lifted the hair away from her cheek.

Talia Larrivee stared up at him, her once lovely features rigid with shock.

Shane left the cabin and found Robby standing in the shade of a clump of aspens. Some of the color had returned to his face. "Did you find her?" he asked.

Shane nodded. "Did you recognize her?"

Robby pressed his lips together. "Maybe," he said after a minute. "But I only looked at her a minute. It was such a shock."

"I'm not asking for a definite identification," Shane said. "But did you think you had seen her before?"

He nodded. "I think she was one of the women I told you about," he said. "With Troy Allen. Not the blonde you showed me the picture of, but the other one."

Shane had suspected as much, but Robby added confirmation. "We'll need to get statements from you and your wife," he said. "And I'll need you to stay here with me until other officers arrive. Then I'll have someone take you back to your home."

"Yes, sir. Can I ask—how did she die? I mean, what was she doing up here—all alone?"

"I don't think she was alone when she died," Shane said.

"Do you mean someone killed her?" Robby's eyes widened.

"I can't say officially," Shane said. He probably shouldn't have said anything at all, but it was too late now.

"I saw the blood," Robby said. "I thought she might have fallen and hit her head."

"I don't think so." Not that he'd seen many gun-shot wounds, but he was pretty sure that was what had killed Talia Larrivee. "We'll let the crime scene experts make that determination. I'm going to ask you not to talk about this with anyone except your wife. The same goes for her."

"We won't say anything," Robby said. "But do you think we need to be worried?" He wiped his mouth. "We've always felt so safe up here. Something like this—it's really shaken us up."

"I don't think you have anything to worry about," Shane said. "But it's always a good idea to be cautious. And if you see anyone suspicious, give us a call."

"We will." He stared toward the road, away from the cabin. "Someone should tell Mr. Kramer."

"You know him?" Shane asked.

"Well, not really know him." He grimaced. "He's not very friendly. But he's our neighbor and we get along okay." He laughed, though it came out more like a cough. "Becca brings him baked goods and stuff from our greenhouse and he likes that. I think we've con-vinced him that we're not after his gold."

"I'll stop by and have a word with him," Shane said. Until they ruled him out, Kramer would be on the list of suspects in Talia's murder. He'd admitted to argu-ing with the group Talia was a part of, and to firing a weapon on them. What if his bullet had struck her, and he'd tried to hide the crime by bringing her body here? He shook his head. He was getting ahead of himself, forgetting his training. First, collect the evidence. Study your findings, then start to develop a theory. Approaching the case any other way was asking for trouble.

LAUREN RAN TO meet the sheriff's department cruiser when it turned into Becca's driveway but drew up short when she realized Shane wasn't behind the wheel. Robby Olsen emerged from the passenger side of the vehicle, and the older man who was driving leaned over and addressed Lauren. "Are you Ms. Baker?" he asked. "Deputy Ellis asked me to give you a ride to your car. He's going to be tied up at the crime scene for a while."

"What's happened?" she asked, looking from Robby, who stood with his arm around Becca, to the older officer. "Who was the woman they found?"

"I don't know, ma'am," the officer said. "I'm a reserve deputy, called in to help shuttle people around and such."

Lauren had been on the edge of panic since Robby had made his startling announcement about finding a woman's body. She didn't think she could bear another minute of suspense. She turned to Robby. "Please, tell me," she said. "Did the woman have blond hair?"

Robby glanced at the officer, then shook his head. "She wasn't a blonde," he said. "Definitely not. But I promised Shane I wouldn't say anything else."

Relief almost buckled Lauren's knees. She swayed a little, then steadied herself. The dead woman wasn't Courtney. She'd confirm that with Shane later, but it was enough for now.

"We should get going," the officer said.

Lauren nodded. "Will you two be all right?" she asked Becca and Robby.

"We'll be fine." Becca forced a smile. "I'm better now that Robby is here. And we have plenty of work to keep us occupied."

"Thank you for waiting with me." She climbed into the cruiser, and the reserve officer executed a Y-turn and sped out of the drive, kicking up a cloud of dust and gravel. "This is the first really big crime we've had since I was hired," the officer said as he turned onto the road. "Most of the time they have me stopping speeders out on the highway or doing traffic control for funerals and things like that. Before Deputy Ellis asked me to transport Mr. Olsen and you, I got to help set up the crime scene barriers and watch the forensics team work."

"What do they think happened to the woman?" Lauren asked.

The officer pursed his lips. "I don't think I'm supposed to say."

"I'll ask Shane later, then," she said. "I'm sure he'll tell me."

"Well, I guess it would be all right to tell you, since you're his friend and all." He glanced at her, eyes alight with excitement. "I overheard a couple of the deputies saying she was shot in the head."

Lauren shuddered. "Do they have any idea who shot her?"

"Not that I heard, but we'll find out, I'm sure. I mean, if she's local, someone will know her, and they'll know who her friends and family are, and probably who her enemies are." He glanced at her again. "Strangers sometimes kill people, but most of the time it's someone the victim knew." He cleared his throat. "At least, that's what they taught us in the academy."

The dead woman isn't Courtney, she reminded herself. Trey or Tom didn't kill her.

But suddenly, it felt more urgent than ever to find her. She couldn't explain why she was so afraid Trey would harm Courtney, but it was a fear she couldn't shake.

The officer dropped her off at her car and headed back toward the crime scene. She drove to her rental, went inside and sank down on the sofa, suddenly too weary to stand. The events of the day, from being held at gunpoint by Von King to Martin Kramer threatening them with a shotgun, to learning that a woman had been murdered in the area where Courtney and Ashlyn had last been seen had drained her emotionally and physically.

Still, she jumped as if hit with an electric shock when her phone buzzed with notification of a text message. She hastily pulled it from her pocket, expecting to see a message from Shane. Instead, she received an even bigger shock when she saw the text was from Courtney.

Stop following me and go back to Denver. I'm fine, and I'm doing what Michael would have wanted. Ash sends her love. Court

She read the message through three times and began to tremble. She hit the button to dial the number and waited with the phone pressed tight to her ear as it rang once, twice…five times. Then silence. Not even a message that the voice mailbox was full. She texted: Court-ney, call me, please.

But no answer came.

She paced the living room, clutching the phone and willing it to ring again. Finally, unable to bear this alone any longer, she sent a text to Shane. I heard from Court-ney. I'm very worried. She says she's okay, but every-thing about the text was ALL WRONG.

SHANE STOOD WITH Travis as two attendants carried Ta-lia's draped body past them to the waiting ambulance. "I'll need to notify Evan Larrivee before word gets out," Travis said.

"Do you want me to come with you?" Shane asked. Notifying a parent their child had been murdered had to be a law enforcement officer's worst duty.

"No, I want you to interview Martin Kramer again. Find out more about his encounter with Talia and the others. Then get back to the station and find out every-thing you can about him. And start the search for the people Talia was last seen with—Tom, Trey Allerton and Courtney Baker. Get their pictures and descriptions to the media and other agencies, and re-interview any-one they spoke to in the last week. Put out a descrip-tion of any vehicles they may have been driving, too."

"You think one of them killed her?" Shane asked.

"I'm not making any assumptions at this point, but if they weren't responsible, I want to know why she wasn't with them when she died. They may know something that will lead us to her killer."

Shane looked around the mine ruins. "Why leave

her here?" he asked. "It's out of the way but it's near a popular hiking trail, and these old ruins get plenty of visitors in the summer and fall."

"Maybe because her killer wanted her found, but not right away," Travis said. "Or because she was killed nearby and the killer was in a hurry to get rid of the body and leave."

"You don't think she was killed here?"

Travis met his gaze. "Do you?"

Shane shook his head. "No. There isn't enough blood, and the body didn't look like someone who had been shot and collapsed. It was more…arranged."

Travis nodded. "I think so, too. If we can find where she was killed, that might help us find the murderer."

"I'm still thinking about that photograph we found in her bedroom," Shane said. "It was hidden very carefully. Talia wanted to keep it, but she didn't want someone coming across it accidentally. Why?"

"Maybe she knew the woman in the photograph," Travis said.

"Or maybe she knew the person who tied up the woman and took the photograph," Shane said. "Maybe she came across the photo and kept it."

Travis nodded. "Go on. Why did she keep it?"

"Blackmail?" Shane guessed. "Or to use if that person tried to harm her?"

The sheriff frowned. "Maybe."

"Maybe her father knows something he isn't saying," Shane said. "Has Talia been in trouble before? Not here, but in other places they lived? Maybe as a minor, or something Larrivee managed to have suppressed?"

"Something that would have put her in contact with the kind of people who would take a picture like that one?" Travis nodded. "The kind of people who might kill her if she threatened to tell what she knew." He pulled his keys from his pocket. "I'll see what I can learn from Larrivee. In the meantime, talk to Kramer and get started on that search."

Martin Kramer didn't come out to greet Shane when the sheriff's department cruiser stopped in front of his shack. Shane waited in the car a moment before getting out, but all around him was still and silent. He emerged cautiously, aware that if Kramer had killed Talia, he might not hesitate to shoot a law enforcement officer who came looking for him.

"Mr. Kramer!" he called. "I need to talk to you again!"

No answer. Shane approached the shack at an angle, one hand on his weapon. He pounded on the door and called for Kramer again. No answer. Shane tried the knob, but it wouldn't budge. Then he noticed the padlock on the outside of the door, slipped through a hasp and fastened. Locked from the outside, so Kramer probably wasn't inside.

He looked around the area, searching the ground for any evidence of blood, or signs of a struggle. He spent some time extending the search far beyond the house but saw nothing out of order, not a broken branch or rock that looked out of place, and nothing that looked like blood. He started to return to the car, then noticed a well-worn path leading away from the house. He followed the path and after several hundred feet saw the black opening of a mine tunnel. As he neared the tunnel, Kramer emerged, a five-gallon bucket of rock in each hand. The old man glowered at Shane. "What are you doing back here?"

"I had some more questions about the four people you shot at a few days ago," Shane said.

Kramer set down the buckets and dusted off his hands. "I didn't shoot at them," he said. "I fired over their heads. I wanted to scare them into leaving me alone."

"Are you sure you didn't hit one of them?" Shane asked. "Maybe the bullet ricocheted off a rock."

"If I had wanted to hit one of them, I would have. But I didn't."

"We found the body of one of the women at the mine ruins off the Sanford Mine trail," Shane said. "She'd been shot in the head."

Kramer recoiled, as if slapped. "Well, I sure as hell didn't shoot her. Which woman? How do you know it was one of the ones I talked to?"

"You said one of the women you saw was a tall redhead?"

"Yeah. So what?"

"This was a tall redhead."

"Well, she was alive and well last time I saw her." He picked up his buckets and pushed past Shane. Shane followed him toward the shack.

"What exactly happened after you fired the shotgun?" he asked.

"The big guy who'd been doing all the talking swore at me and got in the car and the others piled in after him. He peeled out of here, kicking up gravel. I never saw or heard from them again."

"You said if they came back, they'd be sorry. What did you mean by that?"

Kramer set down the buckets again and faced Shane. "Let's just say if they tried to go in the mine, they might end up with a half a ton of rock on top of them."

"You set up a booby trap," Shane said.

"Nobody could prove it wasn't an accident."

"What did you do before you came here to mine, Mr. Kramer?" Shane asked.

"None of your business."

"I can probably find out, so why not tell me?"

"I was a mining engineer. Doesn't matter who for."

"And you just decided to strike out on your own?"

"Some of us don't like working for other people." He picked up the buckets again. "I'm busy here and I'm tired of talking."

Shane let him go. Looking around the place, he had seen no signs of violence, and Kramer's shock at the news that Talia's body had been found seemed genuine—though maybe the man was a good actor. But Shane could find no reason to charge the old man with any crime. Better to collect more evidence and see where it led.

He was halfway to town when his phone sounded a text alert. He'd been out of signal range at the crime scene, and sometimes it took a while for messages to register once he was in range again. He hit the button to have the text read to him.

A mechanical voice indicated the message was from

Lauren. "I heard from Courtney. She says she's okay, but everything about the message is all wrong."

He frowned and thought about pulling over to call and ask what was going on, but decided to wait until he was at the sheriff's department. He'd have a better phone signal and he could make a record of the conversation, as yet more evidence in what was turning out to be a serious case.

LAUREN DIDN'T WAIT for Shane to return her call. She drove to the sheriff's department and was waiting for Shane when he walked through the front door. She rose from the visitor's chair as Adelaide said, "Ms. Baker would like to speak with you, if you're available."

"I got your message." Shane touched Lauren's shoulder. "Come on back. I'll find somewhere we can talk."

They ended up in a small gray room she imagined was usually used to interrogate suspects, but right now privacy was more important than decor. She settled into one of the two chairs at the small square table and tried to ignore the camera and microphone hanging overhead.

"I'll be right back," Shane said. He left and reappeared less than a minute later with two bottles of water and set one in front of her. Then he sank into the adjacent chair. "How are you doing?" he asked.

I'm a mess was too frank a confession for her to make, and admitting as much might be all it took to lead to a meltdown. "I'm upset," she said. "But I need to stay strong, for Courtney and Ashlyn."

"The body we found wasn't Courtney's," he said. "I'm sorry—I should have told you that sooner."

She nodded. "Robby Olsen told me the woman didn't have blond hair. He wouldn't say anything else, but he told me that much. But I've been wondering—was it Talia Larrivee?"

The sudden rigid set of his jaw gave her her answer. "You don't have to tell me, if you can't," she said. "But I'm guessing it was. And the officer who drove me to my car said it was a murder scene. That means Tom or Trey may have killed her. We know she was seen with them."

"We don't know much at this point," he said. "We can't jump to conclusions."

He couldn't. But she could. But she hadn't come here to talk about that. She took out her phone, pulled up the message from Courtney and passed it to him. "That's the text I received from Courtney's number a little while ago," she said.

Shane read it, then laid the phone on the table between them. "She says she's okay. Don't you believe her?"

"Someone wants me to think she's okay," Lauren said. "But Courtney didn't write that message. Or if she did, someone made her get in touch to tell me to back off and she was letting me know the only way she could that she wasn't being sincere."

He frowned. "What makes you say that?"

She turned the phone so that she could read the message. "No one ever called Mike 'Michael.' Not even Courtney. Because his given name isn't Michael. It's Machiel—it's Dutch and it was my mother's father's name." She stabbed a finger at the phone. "She also never referred to Ashlyn as Ash. She hated that. She'd get really upset if anyone called Ashlyn by that nickname. She also hated when anyone called her Court. She would never sign her name that way—unless she was signaling me."

"You think she deliberately used the wrong names in order to let you know something was wrong?"

"Yes." She sat back, relieved that he understood. "I'm really worried. She's not telling me to leave her alone—she's letting me know she needs help."

"Did you try texting her back or calling her?"

"Of course I did. And she didn't answer. She may have been afraid to, with Trey watching her. Or he might have taken the phone away after she sent this message." She leaned toward him again. "Don't you see—this proves what I've been saying all along. Courtney and Ashlyn are in real trouble."

"We'll keep that in mind," he said.

That was it? She'd been expecting more of an answer. "What are you going to do?" she asked.

"We'll continue to search for Courtney and Allerton and Tom," he said.

He hadn't mentioned Talia—further confirmation that hers was the body the Olsens had found. "Can't you trace this text?" she asked. "Use technology to locate Courtney's phone and, we hope, Courtney?"

He pushed the phone toward her. "It's remotely possible that with a lot of time, effort and expense we might be able to determine an approximate location of a tower that transmitted the phone signal. But like everything else, it gets more complicated in the mountains, where towers are far apart and there are big dead spaces. And I'm pretty sure the technicians that do that kind of tracing have to send a message to her phone to do that. If she has it turned off or is in a dead area, they won't get the information they need."

"So what are you going to do?" she asked.

"We'll keep looking. We're going to distribute Allerton's and Tom's and Courtney's descriptions and photographs to other law enforcement agencies and to the media. We're trying to learn Tom's identity and background. We're asking anyone who has information about them to contact us. We're going to re-interview everyone who had contact with them and we're going to put every resource we can into finding them."

"Because you think one of them murdered Talia."

"One of them may know something that will help us find her killer."

She gripped his arm, and his eyes met hers. "If Trey or Tom killed Talia, then Courtney is in danger," she said. "And don't bother saying Courtney might have been involved in murder, because she wouldn't have been."

"She may be in danger," he said. "But we're going to do everything we can to find her."

"What can I do?" she asked.

"Let us know if you hear from Courtney again. Get in touch with her friends and other family and let them know to contact us if they hear from her." His eyes met hers. "I know it can be difficult to keep from thinking up the very worst-case scenario in situations like this, but don't tie yourself in knots that way. We have every reason to believe that Courtney and Ashlyn are still alive and well. Try to focus on that. And know that I will do everything in my power to find them."

She released her grip on him and sat back, drained. "I'll try." She knew he meant everything he said, yet it wasn't enough. But it was the best she could hope for.

Chapter Fourteen

Travis convened everyone involved with investigating Talia Larrivee's murder—most of the small department—at 8:00 the next morning. "I'll start with the medical examiner's report," he said when everyone was assembled around the long conference table. "Talia Larrivee died from a single gunshot wound to the head. The bullet was still lodged in her skull." He held up a clear evidence pouch showing the smashed lump of metal. "Two-twenty-five caliber."

"So not a pistol shot?" Gage asked.

"And not at close range." Travis set the evidence envelope aside. "Dr. Collins estimates she'd been dead approximately ten to fourteen hours when she was found, but she had probably only been in that abandoned cabin four to six hours. Lividity had set in by the time the body was moved. Before that, she lay on her back."

"So she was killed and either left lying where she fell or moved somewhere right away, and then to the mine ruins later," Shane said.

Travis nodded and consulted his tablet once more. "In addition to the gunshot wound, the report notes several recent minor injuries, including bruising on the side of the face, and cuts and scrapes on her palms and knees."

"Could those have happened when she was shot?" Wes Landry, a recent addition to the department, asked. "Maybe she was running away and fell?"

"Maybe," Travis said. "Butch Collins was able to collect some fine gravel from the palms. It looks pretty typical for this area, but I'm going to send it off for analysis." He held up a second evidence pouch.

"It sounds like she was trying to flee her killer and was shot," Dwight said.

"That's consistent with the evidence," Travis said.

"Any luck identifying the man she's been seen with around town?" Gage asked. "Tom?"

"Not yet," Travis said. "Adelaide has a video appointment with a police artist this afternoon to try to come up with a likeness, since she spoke to him at ball practice on Friday. But it would help if we had a photograph."

"Tammy Patterson was at practice," Jamie said. "She had her camera with her and I think she took some photos for the paper. Maybe one of them shows Tom."

"Shane, go talk to her when we're done here," Travis said.

"Yes, sir."

"Here's something else that may or may not help us." Travis tapped his tablet screen. "We have a probable ID for the photograph of the bound woman found in Talia's bedroom. Samantha Morrison, twenty-two, disappeared two years ago from Colorado Springs. Her body was found in the mountains northwest of the city eight months later. El Paso County Sheriff's Department and the Colorado Bureau of Investigation have no leads in the case. They're going to dig a little deeper and get back to me, but nothing in their files shows a link to Trey Allerton, Courtney Baker or anyone named Tom. The only similarity is that her remains were found near the ruins of an old mine."

"It could be the same killer," Gage said.

"Or it could be a coincidence," Travis said. "Colorado is full of old mines, and they make convenient disposal places for a lot of things. But we'll continue to look for other links. And so will other people. Evan Larrivee is offering a one-hundred-thousand-dollar reward for information leading to the apprehension and conviction of his daughter's killer."

Someone let out a low whistle. "That will bring a lot of loonies out of the woodwork," Dwight said.

"But it might bring real evidence, too," Travis said. "Adelaide is setting up a schedule for some of our civilian volunteers to handle phone calls on a hotline number Larrivee has established. We'll have to sift through it all, but maybe something useful will pop up."

The rest of the meeting consisted of presenting the evidence found at the mine site—almost nothing—and updates on an outstanding burglary, a fraud investigation and plans for the upcoming Fourth of July festivities.

"Maybe we shouldn't have the ball game this year," Shane said. "It might look like we're not taking this murder seriously."

"I spoke to Evan Larrivee about that," Travis said.

"He said he's okay with the game continuing, since the money it raises goes to the Little League program. The organization relies on that money each year."

"And if we back out, we'll never hear the end of it from the fire department," Gage said. "But we may have to shorten our practice time."

"That shouldn't hurt us," Dwight said. "Not with Shane on the mound. Everybody knows pitching wins games."

If anyone saw Shane wince, they didn't remark on it. As soon as the meeting ended, he headed for the newspaper office.

Reporter Tammy Patterson looked up from her desk as Shane approached. "Hey, there!" she said, all smiles. An energetic woman with curly brown hair and wide hazel eyes, Tammy was a familiar visitor to the sheriff's department. "I got some great shots of you pitching the other night. Want to see?"

"I would like to see the pictures you took the other night," he said. "But not the ones of me."

"Oh?" She indicated the chair beside her desk. "Have a seat and fill me in."

"I'm looking for any photos you have of the man Talia Larrivee was with," he said.

Tammy's smile vanished. "It's so horrible, what happened to her. Mr. Larrivee came in first thing this morning to drop off her obituary and to take out a big ad. He's offering a reward for information that leads to finding Talia's murderer."

"Did you speak to her Friday at the practice?" Shane asked.

Tammy shook her head as she typed on her computer keyboard. "I knew her, but we didn't run in the same circles. I saw the guy she was with, though."

"What did you think?"

She made a face. "I thought he was too old for her, and pretty rough looking, but she had a thing for bad boys—hard partiers and risk takers. I think maybe she did it to upset her dad. I mean, can you imagine? I don't guess any father wants his daughter hanging out with lowlifes, but the Larrivees are rich—high-society types."

"Talia dated ex-cons? Who?"

"Oh, she wasn't with the guy very long. I ran into them at the park last summer and she introduced me and made a point of telling me the guy had just got out of prison—like I should be impressed or something."

"Do you remember his name?"

"No. Is it important?" Her eyes widened. "Oh, wow. Do you think her ex-con ex might have come back to murder her?"

"It would be helpful if I had a name to check out."

"I honestly can't remember, but maybe one of Talia's friends will. She has a couple of women she seems pretty tight with."

"I'll ask them about him. Thanks. Now about that picture."

"Sure. Here's the file with all the shots I took that evening. Let's see what I have."

She began scrolling through the photos. She paused at one of Shane in the middle of his windup. "You've still got it," she said. "Want me to print you a copy?"

"No, thanks." He studied his form critically. He'd put on a few pounds since retiring. His leg kick wasn't as high, and he didn't have as much power. Most people probably didn't see those flaws, but they stood out to him.

Tammy scrolled through a few more photos, then stopped at one of Talia Larrivee and an older olive-skinned man with thick black hair. Tom had a dark five-o'clock shadow and a heavy brow, and he was frowning. "He doesn't look very friendly, does he?" Tammy said.

Shane studied the people around Talia and Tom. All locals—no one who might be Trey Allerton or Courtney Baker.

"Can you blow that up and crop it so it just shows him?" he asked.

"Sure." She did as he asked. "How many copies do you want?"

"Can you send the digital file to the sheriff's office?" He wrote the address on the back of one of his cards and passed it to her.

"No problem." She typed in the address and hit Send, then turned back to him. "Do you think this guy killed Talia?"

"We need to talk to him," he said.

"Well, I hope this helps." She grabbed a reporter's notebook and a pen from beside the computer. "What can you tell me about the case so far? I have the statement the sheriff sent over, but it's a little dry. There's not much detail."

"That's because we don't have much detail yet."

"Come on, Shane. Help me out here. This is a big

story and all I have is that Talia's body was found yesterday up at the old Sanford Mine ruins by unnamed hikers. Mr. Larrivee told me she'd been shot in the head. And I know law enforcement are searching for three people Talia might have been with." She plucked a piece of paper from a box at the corner of her desk. "Courtney Baker, Trey Allerton and a man named Tom." She nodded to the computer screen. "I'm assuming that's Tom."

"Yes. But that's all I have for you, Tammy." He stood.

"Who were the hikers?" she asked.

"I'm pretty sure they don't want to talk about the experience."

"What about Courtney Baker? Is she related to Lauren Baker? I've seen the two of you around together a lot lately."

He sighed. "Courtney was married to Lauren's late brother. And that's all I'm going to say." He turned to leave.

"I'm going to call Lauren and ask for an interview," Tammy said.

"You do that." Maybe Lauren would appreciate the opportunity to talk about Courtney to a larger audience. He hadn't been much help to her so far. He knew she was frustrated by the lack of progress in finding her brother's widow. Maybe she even believed he didn't care. But as a law enforcement officer, he couldn't let emotion get in the way of an investigation. His training had drilled into him the importance of following procedures and being methodical. Put together a strong case and things worked out better for everyone.

He sent Lauren a text, letting her know to expect a

call from Tammy, then returned to the office to find the sheriff studying the photo of Tom. "I'll send this off to the other law enforcement offices in the state, and to the FBI," Travis said. "If we're lucky, someone will recognize him."

"How often do we get lucky like that?" Shane asked.

Travis shook his head. "Not nearly often enough."

LAUREN WAS A little nervous about talking to a reporter, but Tammy Patterson quickly put her at ease. The two met at Lauren's rental, and Tammy arrived with two iced coffees and a bag of bakery cookies. "This isn't a bribe," she said, as she handed over one of the coffees. "I didn't have time for breakfast this morning, so you get to share while we talk."

The two settled on the sofa, and Lauren showed Tammy the photograph of Courtney and Ashlyn. "Your niece is adorable," Tammy said. "And Courtney is gorgeous. People should remember if they've seen her."

"A few people have seen her with Trey Allerton, and once with Trey and Talia Larrivee and a man named Tom."

"Shane told me about Tom," Tammy said. "He stopped by the paper this morning to pick up a photo I took of Talia and Tom at ball practice the other night. That's when I made the connection between Courtney Baker and you."

"I wish I had been at that practice," Lauren said.

"So tell me about your sister-in-law," Tammy said. "What is she like?"

For the next half hour, Tammy listened and took

notes while Lauren talked about Courtney's sweetness, how much she loved her late husband and her daughter, and about how Lauren believed she had been manipulated by Trey Allerton. "I understand that it's only natural for Courtney to find someone to love again. I want that for her. It would be great for her to not be alone, and for Ashlyn to have a dad. But Trey Allerton doesn't love her. He's only using her for her money."

"What about Tom?" Tammy asked. "Where does he come in?"

"I don't know. But everyone who saw him with them said Tom looked rough. Samuel Russell said he thought he was an ex-con. I guess he recognized prison tattoos or something. And now Talia has been murdered." She shuddered. "I'm just really worried about Courtney. She's the type who sees good in everyone."

"What about Shane?" Tammy asked.

The question startled her. "What do you mean?"

"What does he think has happened to Courtney?"

"He doesn't know. Or if he does, he isn't telling me."

"I've seen you with him a lot around town," Tammy said.

"He's been helping me track Courtney's movements."

"I'm a regular at the sheriff's department and I haven't seen anything about that on their list of ongoing cases," Tammy said.

"It wasn't an official investigation," Lauren admitted. "Until now. Now that she and Trey have been linked to Talia Larrivee, everyone is getting a lot more serious about looking for her."

"So Shane was helping you look for her, unofficially?" Tammy asked.

"Yes."

"He's a nice guy," Tammy said. "And a really good-looking one. And it seems like he takes his job as a deputy really serious. Not a second career I would have expected from a former Major Leaguer, but it seems to suit him."

"I never followed baseball," Lauren said.

"Maybe he likes that." Tammy bit into a cookie and chewed, looking thoughtful. "Maybe Shane is attracted to you because you accept him for who he is, not who he was."

"Oh, I don't think he's attracted to me." Even as she made the protest, her cheeks grew hot, and she remembered Shane's kiss.

Tammy laughed. "Oh, he's into you, all right. I've seen the way he looks at you."

Lauren's heart beat faster. "How does he look at me?"

"I'm no expert, but I'd say when Shane looks at you, he looks exactly like a man in love."

PRACTICE TUESDAY EVENING for their upcoming charity baseball game was meant to be a low-key affair, a brief break from the more pressing business of investigating a murder. The players had all agreed that they wouldn't invite friends and family to attend, and that they would keep it brief and businesslike.

So Shane was surprised to see Lauren on the third base sideline, talking with Adelaide. "Hello," he greeted her while waiting for practice to begin. "I didn't think you liked baseball."

"Adelaide told me I needed to be here," Lauren said.

"There's no sense sitting around that rental apartment fretting," Adelaide said. She shook her head, her earrings—were those French poodles?—jangling. "I gave her a ride here—I figure you can take her home."

He'd have to pull the office manager aside some time and let her know he didn't need her help with women. He wondered what Lauren thought of such blatant matchmaking, but a quick read of her expression revealed a pleased look. That was certainly interesting.

"Shane, we need you on the mound." Gage had agreed to serve as their player coach, and he was organizing the team for a batting drill. Shane headed for the mound.

Gage walked out to the mound a minute later. "Kerry Swearingham, the pitcher for the firehouse team, only has one pitch," he said. "A fastball he likes to throw up and in to get guys off the plate. So give us a lot of that for now."

Shane nodded and rubbed up the ball. He could throw fastballs all night. Some of his fellow officers might even be good enough to hit one, but on game day he'd be giving the fire crew a steady diet of breaking balls and rockets. They'd be begging for the game to end.

As it was, his fellow deputies were talking trash about them by the third batter. "Come on, Shane," Dwight complained. "This is supposed to be batting practice. Give us something we can hit."

"You can hit this stuff," Shane said. "I'm not even throwing hard." It was true. His arm felt great, but he wasn't putting that much power behind these pitches. His professional teammates would have laughed him out of the dugout if he'd thrown this slow stuff to them.

Dwight ended up fouling off three pitches in a row, then it was Nate Hall's turn. The husband of Deputy Jamie Douglas, Nate was helping to fill out the team roster.

Shane glanced toward the sidelines and saw Lauren deep in conversation with a man in a sheriff's department uniform. That reserve deputy—Anderson. Wasn't he supposed to be on duty tonight?

"Are you gonna pitch or just stand there?" Gage called.

Shane forced his attention back to the game. He wound up and threw one straight down the middle.

Lauren laughed, and he looked over to see her leaning toward Anderson, who was grinning. What did the two of them find so funny?

Crack! Nate's bat connected with Shane's fastball, sending it hurtling back toward the mound.

"Shane!" someone shouted.

He started to turn, then was knocked sideways by the impact of the ball on the side of his helmet. He went down, tried to get up, then was lost to a wave of darkness.

Chapter Fifteen

Lauren didn't remember screaming. She didn't remember racing onto the field, though later people told her she had done both those things. She wasn't aware of anything until she was kneeling on the ground beside Shane's body, both hands on his chest, staring down at his very pale, very still face.

"The ball hit him on the side of the head." Gage stood over them. "He went down like a tree."

"Get that helmet off of him." The sheriff knelt beside them and reached for Shane's head.

Lauren put out a hand to stop him. "Wait," she said. "There could be injury to his neck or spine. Don't touch his head until we're sure."

Travis stared at her.

"I'm a nurse practitioner," she said. "I know what I'm talking about."

Travis nodded. "Somebody call 911," he said.

Shane moaned, and Lauren leaned over him. His heart beat strong beneath her palm and he was breathing, if a little labored. "Shane, it's Lauren," she said. "You were hit by a ball."

"You got in the way of my home run." The batter, with a female deputy beside him, hovered near. The young man shifted his gaze to Lauren. "Is he going to be all right?"

"I'm fine." Shane tried to sit up, even as Lauren pushed at his chest.

"Don't move," she commanded. "The ambulance is on the way." At least, she hoped that was true.

"Why do I need an ambulance when I have you?" Shane said. But he lay back down and closed his eyes. He was very pale, and his skin was clammy.

A list of worst-case scenarios, from fractured skull to internal bleeding, ran through Lauren's mind. He was right—they didn't need to wait for an ambulance when she had the capability of doing an initial assessment right now. "Does anyone have a flashlight I can borrow?" she asked.

"You can use mine." Chuck Anderson slipped his from his duty belt and extended it to her. Chuck had been with her on the sidelines when Shane was hit. Chuck had been telling her a funny story about a traffic stop he had made earlier in the day. The man was driving with a boa constrictor coiled around one arm because, as the man explained, "My snake likes to look out the window when we're driving around."

"Open your eyes, Shane," Lauren said.

He opened them, and she shone the light in each one, the pupils contracting as they should. "How do you feel?" she asked.

"My head hurts, and there's a rock digging into the small of my back."

"You ever get hit by a line drive when you were playing pro ball?" Gage asked.

"In the arm and chest a few times," Shane said. "Never in the head. But I saw it happen to other guys. Can I sit up now? I'm fine, really."

"Slowly," Lauren said, and took his hand.

He sat and put a hand to his head, blinking. "That really rang my bell." He took off the helmet and probed at the area around his temple. "I bet I have a beauty of a bruise there by tomorrow," he said.

The wail of an ambulance grew gradually louder. Shane groaned. "You didn't have to call the ambulance."

"Better to make sure you don't have a concussion," Travis said.

"I was wearing a helmet," Shane said. "I'm fine."

"Let them check you out, just to be sure," Lauren said.

He met her gaze, then nodded—and winced at the movement.

"Coming through!" A female paramedic pushed through the crowd around the pitcher's mound, followed by an older man. She stopped in front of Shane. "Who beaned you?" she asked.

"He's the one who threw the ball right over the plate and didn't get out of the way," the batter protested.

"You have to make sure he's okay to pitch in Sunday's game," someone at the back of the crowd called.

Lauren stood and offered a hand to the paramedic. "I'm Lauren Baker," she said. "I'm a nurse practitioner. I did a preliminary exam and his vitals are good, pupils normal, no sign of fracture or external bleeding."

"Merrily Rayford." The paramedic shook her hand.

"And that's Emmett Baxter." She indicated her partner, then dropped to her knees in the dirt beside Shane. "Let's see what we've got here."

Fifteen minutes later, Merrily sat back and began packing her gear. "You check out okay, but you need to have your skull x-rayed to rule out fracture or an internal bleed. We can transport you or you can have someone else drive you."

"I'll take him." Lauren and Travis spoke at the same time.

"I'll go with Lauren," Shane said.

"The rest of you, get back out there," Gage said. "We'll work on our fielding."

A chorus of grumbling gradually receded as the others took their positions around the ballfield. Travis remained behind. "Do you need anything else?" he asked when Shane was on his feet and standing beside Lauren.

"I'm fine," Shane said. "Lauren will take good care of me."

His words, and the trust they implied, sent warmth spreading through her. Travis started to turn away, and she came out of her dreamy fog enough to say, "There is one thing, Sheriff."

Travis turned back toward them, waiting.

Lauren flushed. "Could you give us a ride to my rental? My car is there."

Shane laughed, and even the sheriff looked like he might smile. "Come on," he said. "Let's get you two out of here."

SHANE HATED HOSPITALS and tests and paperwork and being fussed over. But he put up with it, because if you were an athlete, that was what you did. Even minor injuries had to be checked out so that they didn't turn into something major. Because of that, he figured he had had most major body parts x-rayed at some point in his career that spanned from Little League to the majors.

"Looks like your helmet and your hard head saved you," the emergency room doctor pronounced two hours after Shane and Lauren's arrival at the hospital in Junction. Lauren was with him in the little exam cubicle, perched on a folding chair and studying the images of Shane's brain projected on a monitor an aid had rolled in. "You'll probably have some bruising and a headache. If anything else develops, see your regular physician." The ER doctor turned to Lauren. "You know what to look for, but I don't anticipate any problems."

"I'll keep an eye on him," she said, with a proprietary tone he thought he could get used to.

"Are you tired?" she asked when they were in her car again, headed back toward Eagle Mountain.

"I'm starving." He hadn't eaten before practice, not liking to play on a full stomach.

"What do you want to eat?" she asked.

"A cheeseburger. A really good one. And I know just the place."

He directed her to a combination bait shop, convenience store and grill by the river, where they ate cheeseburgers and fries on benches beneath leafy cottonwoods, bathed in the glow of lights strung through the branches. "I can't believe I pitched for three years to guys who were probably trying to hit me, and a fellow sheriff's deputy ends up taking me out," he said.

"How's your head?" she asked.

"I have a headache, but I don't want to talk about it."

"All right. What do you want to talk about?"

"What do you think about coming back to my place and spending the night?" Might as well come right out with it.

She blinked. "Of course. It would be a good idea to have someone with you, until you're sure you're okay."

"I'm not talking about playing nursemaid." He met and held her gaze, wanting no room for misinterpretation. "I want to know if you want to spend the night with me. In my bed. Not sleeping."

The color that flooded her cheeks was something to behold, like a suddenly blooming rose. "Oh." It was a breathy sound, like a woman might make during lovemaking. It didn't sound to him like a rejection. He took her hand. "I figure we've been dancing around the question since we kissed," he said. "So I thought I'd throw it out there."

"I don't know what to think," she said.

He stroked the back of her hand with his thumb. "Don't think. Tell me how you feel."

"All right." She stood, both hands on the table in front of her, and leaned toward him. When her lips met his, he reached for her, and she kissed him with an intensity that had him reeling as much as that line drive. When she broke the kiss, she was smiling. "Yes," she said. "Yes, I want to come with you. And spend the night. Not sleeping."

THEY RETURNED TO Shane's home, and once inside, he wrapped his arms around her and kissed her with an intensity that had every nerve buzzing with anticipation and need. "Tell me if I'm moving too fast," he said when they finally parted.

"You're not moving too fast for me." She leaned in for another kiss, which led to hands exploring each other's bodies. Clothing began to come off as they moved toward the bedroom.

She had the impression of dark furniture and comfortable surfaces as they eased onto the bed. She reached for him again and felt the lump at the side of his head where the ball had struck and for the first time remembered all that had led up to this moment. "How's your head?" she asked. "Are you feeling all right?"

"My head is fine and I'm feeling great." He began kissing along the top of her bra, tracing her cleavage with his tongue. "You feel pretty amazing, too."

"Uh-huh." It was all she could manage as he slipped off her bra and shaped his hands to her breasts, the pressure and heat of his touch magnifying every sensation.

They helped each other out of their remaining clothing and slid under the covers. They lay on their sides, facing each other, resting a moment, hands idly stroking, each taking in the other. "You're beautiful," he murmured, as he slid his hand along the curve of her hip.

"You're gorgeous." She had never been with a man who was so physically perfect, with the toned body of an athlete and the musculature of a man who spent a lot of time in the gym. "I guess being a baseball player required you to stay in shape," she said.

"It's pretty useful for a sheriff's deputy, too." He kissed the top of her shoulder as he slid his hand down, over her stomach and between her legs. She moaned with pleasure as his fingers gently traced the folds of her labia and began to stroke.

"Do you like that?" he murmured.

"Can't you tell?" She nipped at his earlobe.

He laughed, a low rumble that vibrated through her. She slid her hand down his stomach, taking her time tracing each defined ridge of his abdomen, pausing before stroking his erection, delighted by the low sigh he let out when she grasped him. "I hope you have a condom." She took it for granted that he was the kind of responsible man who would, but she'd been wrong about men before.

"Yeah. Hang on." He rolled away and opened the drawer of the bedside table and retrieved a packet. She lay back and closed her eyes, listening as he tore open the packet, breathing in the scent of cotton sheets and aroused man and some lingering memory of his aftershave. *I want to remember this moment*, she thought. *This instant before everything changes.* She hoped the changes would be good ones—she wasn't going to let worry over what might happen in the future ruin the now. She had done that too often in her life. Now was enough, and she was going to enjoy it.

Shane rolled over and reached for her again. She moved confidently with him, delighted when he urged her on top of him. "I like looking up at you," he said as she straddled him. "And I like being able to do this." He cupped her breasts, then began to stroke her nipples, sending shockwaves of sensation through her, escalat-

ing the tension within her, until she was impatient to
be even closer to him.

He had already sheathed himself, and she slid onto
him, wanting to savor the sensation of him filling her
but driven to movement. He grasped her hips, guiding her, and they soon found a rhythm they both enjoyed. She closed her eyes, arched her back and let the
sensations wash over her, his body in hers, his hands
on her hips, her hands on his chest and shoulders, the
taste of him when she bent to kiss him, the way his
muscles contracted with each thrust, the crazy, spi-
raling need that drove her to move faster, sink deeper
and want more.

She shuddered with the force of her orgasm, fingers
digging into his shoulders, holding herself still as the
delicious sensation filled her. He waited with her, holding her a long, breathless moment, before beginning to
move beneath her, driven by his own need. She opened
her eyes and found him looking up at her, the wonder
of the moment reflected back at her. Then they moved
together again, and she felt him come beneath her, a
moment of fulfillment and power that never failed to
make her marvel, just a little.

Eventually, she slid off of him and lay on her side
again, her head on his shoulder, his arm around her in
a gesture that felt so protective and tender and right.
"You're very quiet," he said after a while. "Are you
okay?"

"I'm okay." She shifted so she could kiss his cheek.
"I'm happy—something I haven't been for a very long
time. Since Mike died, I think. Thank you for that."

"You're welcome." His arm tightened around her. "When I said what I did at the restaurant, I half expected you to tell me off for not listening to you when you said you didn't want a relationship."

"Why didn't you listen?" she asked.

"Because, while I'm sure you believed you didn't want a relationship, I think part of you had a very different idea. And I really wanted to be with you. I had to take the risk."

"I'm glad you did."

"What changed your mind?" he asked.

"Maybe with so many bad things happening, I wanted one good thing to focus on." She reached up and touched the side of his face. "Or maybe seeing you get hit by that ball made me rethink my priorities. Or maybe it was seeing—really seeing—the way you look at me."

"How do I look?" he asked.

"Like someone I could trust," she said. Would he think she was being corny? Or be hurt that she couldn't say more? She wanted to say *Like someone I could love*, but she wasn't ready for that yet. She had used those words too lightly in the past, and they had come back to hurt her.

He smiled, and the warmth in that smile spread through her and she lay down again, not wanting him to see the sudden tears. "I'm glad you trust me," he said. "I'll do my best to never let you down."

Never was a long time, but she liked that he thought that way. Maybe one day she'd be able to make that leap, too.

THE PHONE WOKE Shane from deep slumber. Beside him, Lauren stirred. "What time is it?" she murmured.

He lifted his head to check the clock. "Seven thirty." The phone continued to ring, and it took him two tries to find it in the pocket of his pants on the floor beside the bed. The sheriff's number on the screen was like a bucket of cold water dumped over him. Awake now, he sat up on the side of the bed. "Hello?"

"We got a positive ID on that photo of Tom you got from the newspaper," Travis said. As usual, he got right to the point. "His name is Tom Chico and he's been in and out of prison for the past twenty years, for everything from armed robbery to rape."

"Any idea how he hooked up with Trey Allerton?" Shane asked.

"No, but he was living in Woodland Park when Samantha Morrison disappeared."

"That's not far from Colorado Springs," Shane said.

"Not far," Travis agreed. "I'm going to send his information to the police there and see what they come up with. Are you coming in this morning?"

"Yes, sir."

"Head's okay, then?"

"I'm fine." He still had a dull headache, but nothing a cup of strong coffee and two aspirin wouldn't cure.

"See you then," Travis said, and hung up.

Shane turned to find Lauren sitting up also, covers tucked under her arms, watching him. "Did you ever hear Courtney or Trey mention someone named Tom Chico?" he asked.

"No. Is that the Tom who was with Talia Larrivee?"

"We think so. And Mr. Russell was right—he's an ex-con." He flung back the covers. "I have to get to the office." He started to get up, then turned back to her. "Not that I wouldn't rather stay here in bed with you, but this is important."

"Of course it is," she said. "Go. I've got my car, so I can get back to my place all right."

He leaned over and kissed her. "I'll call you later."

"Let me know what you find out. I hate to think of a man with a prison record with Courtney and Ashlyn."

It wasn't the romantic goodbye he had hoped for. But Lauren wasn't with him because he was especially romantic. She had said she trusted him. He needed to work now, to live up to that trust.

Chapter Sixteen

Lauren didn't know what she thought Martin Kramer could tell her that he hadn't already told Shane and the other deputies, but she hoped if she came to see him by herself, without a gun or a lot of men in uniform around, he might trust her with details he hadn't wanted to reveal to law enforcement. If such details even existed. But she owed it to Courtney to keep searching. Shane and his fellow officers were looking for her, too, but only as she related to Talia Larrivee's murder. They were focused on finding Tom Chico, and if he wasn't with Trey and Courtney anymore, they might decide finding Courtney wasn't that important. So Wednesday after Shane left, she headed for the Full Moon Mine.

She stopped first at the trailer on the section of the Russell Ranch that Trey Allerton had leased. She parked in front of the battered structure and studied it for several minutes. The place looked even more derelict than it had on her previous visits, the grimy windows vacant, the wooden steps sagging. A gust of wind sent a dust devil dancing across the dried grass that passed for a front yard.

After a while, she got out of the car and climbed the

steps, but the front door was locked. She cupped her hands around her eyes and tried to see inside, but the small glass pane in the door was so dirty she could only make out dark smudges. Nothing moved in her field of vision, and she was sure the place was unoccupied.

Back in her car, she drove on, past the Olsens' yurt. Becca Olsen, who was working in the garden behind the yurt, straightened and watched as Lauren drove past, but she gave no indication that she recognized the car or driver.

The turnoff to the mine was farther than Lauren remembered, but maybe that was only because the condition of the road forced her to slow to a crawl, guiding the car through deep ruts and around large rocks. When she finally reached the drive leading up to Kramer's shack, with its signs warning her to Keep Out! her heart was beating hard in her chest, and she almost turned back.

But no. She had come this far. She might as well talk to the old man, even if he didn't want to see her. She stopped in front of the shack and waited. Silence enveloped her, broken only by the ping of the engine cooling. Nothing moved around her, yet she had the feeling she wasn't alone.

"What do you want!"

The sudden question startled a scream from her. Kramer had emerged out of nowhere to stand beside her car, the shotgun cradled in his arms. She lowered the driver's window. "You startled me," she said, glaring at him.

He laughed. "I know a thing or two about sneaking up on people," he said. "Learned it in 'Nam." His expression grew serious again. "You're that lady cop who was here the other day with the other one, aren't you?"

"I'm not a cop," she said. "I'm just a woman who is worried about a friend. Can I get out so we can talk?"

"Move slow, and keep your hands where I can see them."

She did as he asked, leaving the keys in the ignition. "I'm not armed," she said. "I only want to know if you've seen my sister-in-law, Courtney, again. She was the pretty blonde with the little girl."

"I've had so many people traipsing through here lately I can't keep track of them all. I had to run a bunch off earlier this morning. So far, I've just been firing over their heads, but a man's got a right to defend his property."

"Who were these people?" she asked.

"I didn't bother asking for identification. I just told them to get out of here."

"Were they men or women? Young or old? How many were there?"

"Are you sure you're not a cop? You ask questions like one."

"Was a blonde woman with any of the people who trespassed on your property?" she asked, desperate for information, but not wanting to make him any angrier.

"I didn't get a good look at all of them. Maybe she was, maybe she wasn't."

Did he truly not know, or was he just being difficult?

She opened his mouth to say as much when a loud report from across the ridge startled her. She started to turn, but Kramer grabbed her arm and shoved her to the ground. "Get under the car!" he ordered. "Now!"

Another report sounded, and she realized someone was shooting at them. She scrambled under the car and lay flat. Kramer crouched beside the car and aimed over the hood. The blast of his shotgun rang in her ears, followed by a metallic thud. With growing horror, she realized a bullet had struck her car. "Why is this happening?" she shouted over the blast of Kramer's shotgun.

His answer was a stream of swearing, then he leaped up and ran from behind the car, toward the gunfire. She thought she heard the shotgun blast again, then answering shots. What if Kramer was hit? Or killed, even? Then the shooter would come after her. Could she get into the car and drive away before they reached her? She told herself she needed to get out from under the car and try, but fear paralyzed her.

While she was struggling with these thoughts, silence descended again. No gunfire, no shouting, no sound of running feet. After what seemed like a long while, Kramer returned. She didn't hear his footsteps, but she saw his boots and the legs of his overalls as he reached the car. He leaned down to look at her. "You can come out now," he said. "I think I scared them off."

Shakily, she crawled out from under the car and stood, and brushed dirt from her clothing. "Who was that?" she asked. "And why were they shooting at us?"

"I don't know who it was. I told you, I've had people up here at all hours of the day and night, harassing me."

"Have you reported this to the police?"

He snorted. "And what are they going to do about it? Anyway, there have been cop cars up and down this road all day long since they found that woman's body at the Sanford Mine. Hasn't kept this bunch from coming after me."

"But why would these people shoot at you?"

"They're trying to steal my claim. But I'm not going to let them. I'm a lot tougher than I look."

He looked pretty tough to her. "How long has this been going on?" she asked.

"Since you people were up here the other day. They've got a lot of nerve, I tell you."

"Do you think any of the people who are after you are the same men who visited you the day you saw Courtney and the dark-haired woman who was killed?"

"I already told you, I haven't got a good look at any of them. It might be the same bunch, and it might not. Seems like there are more of them. But maybe they recruited help." He took a step back. "You better go now. I've got work to do."

"Do you still have the card Deputy Ellis gave you?" she asked.

"I might have it around here somewhere."

"If you see the blonde woman, Courtney, or her little girl, Ashlyn, call the deputy. It's really important."

He shook his head. "Can't do it."

"Why not?"

"I don't have a phone. Go on now. I've wasted enough time talking."

He stood cradling the shotgun, watching as she turned her car and headed back down the driveway. Lauren spent the trip back to town replaying the events of the morning. The sudden shots, the return fire—then all was quiet again. It was surreal, but then, so much of this whole ordeal since Courtney had left Denver didn't make any sense.

ANNE-MARIE WINSTEAD JONES had spent the past week ignoring Shane's phone calls and refusing to answer the door when he stopped by her house. He finally parked around the corner from the very modern steel-and-glass townhome where she lived and waited until she stepped out the front door. She was a tall woman with a fall of thick dark hair and a thin, angular figure. "Ms. Winstead Jones, I need to speak with you," he said, intercepting her as she headed toward the bright green Mercedes GT parked in the drive.

She whipped her head around to stare at him, then picked up her pace. "I can't talk now," she said. "I have an appointment."

He deftly stepped in front of her. "You can answer a few questions now, or I will put you in my cruiser and take you to the sheriff's department and question you there," he said.

"You can't do that," she said. "I haven't done anything wrong."

"I'm investigating a woman's murder—your friend's murder," he said. "And I need your help. If you won't voluntarily help, I can compel you to do so, though I'd rather not."

She jiggled her keys in her hand, a bright silver *A* on the fob glinting in the afternoon sun. "All right," she said after a long moment. She turned back toward the house. "You might as well come inside."

The inside of the condo matched the outside—white leather sofas, white fur rugs, chrome end tables and chairs, and everywhere a view of the mountains from the expanses of glass. Shane's first thought was that it was like living in a snow scene. In the winter it must be freezing.

Anne-Marie sank onto one of the sofas and waved toward a nearby chair. "Have a seat. What do you want to know?" She opened a drawer in the table in front of her, took a cigarette from a silver box and lit it with a crystal lighter.

"Why have you been avoiding me?" he asked.

"Why are you surprised that I don't want to talk about my best friend's death?" She folded one arm across her stomach and took a long drag on the cigarette.

"When was the last time you saw Talia Larrivee?" Shane asked.

"We had lunch last Thursday. We had lunch every Thursday. And we went shopping." She blinked rapidly, eyes shining with unshed tears.

Talia had died on Sunday. "Did you talk to her after that? Text her?"

"I texted her, but she didn't answer." She took another pull on the cigarette, her expression obscured by the sudden exhalation of smoke.

"When did you text her?" Shane asked.

She balanced the cigarette on the rim of a crystal ashtray on the coffee table and shifted to pull out a phone in a pearlescent white case. She tapped the screen with one white-tipped fingernail and scrolled. "I texted her

Friday afternoon, Friday night, Saturday night and Sunday afternoon."

"Let me see." He held out his hand and she passed over the phone.

The messages started off simply enough: Pool this afternoon? I'll make margaritas.

Half an hour later: Come on in, the water is great.

Twenty minutes after that: Whassup girl? Why aren't you answering your phone?

The rest of the messages, sent over the next few days, were increasingly more agitated, varying pleas to know why Talia wasn't responding, ending with a single profane epithet. "You tried to call her, too?" Shane asked. He returned the phone.

"I tried, but it went straight to voice mail," Anne-Marie said. "At first I left messages, but she ignored those, too."

"What did you think had happened?"

She shrugged and picked up the cigarette again. "I figured she was with her new boyfriend, ignoring everyone else. He struck me as that type, you know?"

"Who was he?" Shane asked. "And what type do you mean?"

"The controlling type. The type who wants all the focus on him. She'd already blown me off a couple of times before when I wanted to go out, telling me Tom wouldn't like it." She crushed out the cigarette in the crystal dish. "I don't know who he was, really. I only met him once and I wasn't impressed."

"Tom who?"

"I never heard his last name. Talia went through a lot

of men. I didn't bother getting to know most of them. I didn't want to know this one."

"Tell me about him," Shane said.

"He was almost as old as her father and he was really rough."

"What do you mean 'rough'?"

"He just..." She stared up at the ceiling, as if searching for the right words. Then she met Shane's gaze again. "You know how some young guys have this cocky attitude, all bravado and swagger? They're not really tough, but they pretend to be. Usually it's because they're so insecure. It's easy to see right through it. But with Tom it wasn't an act. Everything about him was a little crude—bad tattoos and cheap clothes." She shuddered. "He felt...dangerous. He scared me, really." She brushed a lock of hair off her forehead. "I think he scared Talia a little, too, but she liked that."

"She liked men who scared her?"

"Yeah. A little."

"So she'd dated men like Tom before?"

"Not exactly like him. But she had a boyfriend once who she told me liked to tie her up and choke her when they were having sex. It kind of freaked me out. I told her she needed to dump him right away, but she just laughed. She said she knew what she was doing. And I guess she did, because a few weeks later, he was out of the picture and she was dating some mountain climber who talked her into going skydiving with him."

"Do you know where the man who tried to choke her is now?"

"No way." She frowned. "I kept waiting for her to

ditch Tom, but she didn't show any signs of losing interest in him."

"Did she mention anything Tom did that was dangerous?"

"Nothing specific." Her gaze shifted away.

"But?" he prompted. There was something, he was sure.

"I asked her once what she saw in him. It was one of the times after she blew me off when I wanted the two of us to go out to a club. She said he was exciting and being with him made her feel so alive and powerful. I told him he scared me and she said I didn't need to worry about her, because she had an insurance policy if he ever stepped out of line."

"What did she mean by that?"

Anne-Marie shook her head. "She wouldn't say, but I kind of took it to mean she knew something she could use to blackmail him. Just from some other things she said. I told her that was a screwed-up way to manage a relationship, but she said that was the only kind she was good at." She looked at the drawer that held the cigarette box, as if contemplating having another.

"Tell me if you've ever seen this before." Shane took out a copy of the photograph he and Travis had found in Talia's room.

Anne-Marie took it and studied the photo of the bound woman. "This isn't Talia," she said. She handed it back to him. "I don't know who it is. What does it have to do with Talia?"

"That was found in her room after she went missing. It's a photograph of a woman who disappeared in Colorado Springs two years ago."

"Why would Talia have something like that?"

"I don't know. I was hoping you would know."

She puzzled over this, forehead creased. "Do you think she got that photograph from Tom? That that was her insurance policy?" She hugged her arms across her stomach. "Do you think that's why he killed her?"

"We don't know who killed her," Shane said.

"The minute I heard she'd been found dead, I knew he did it," she said. "If you had ever met him, you'd know it, too." Her eyes welled with tears again, and this time they spilled over, sliding down her cheeks. "Poor Talia. She was so smart about so many things, but so dumb about men. She thought danger was the same as excitement, even though I tried to tell her it wasn't."

LAUREN WAS STILL debating whether to tell Shane about her visit with Martin Kramer when he came to see her later that evening. When she answered the door, he was frowning. "What happened to your car?" he asked. "It looks like someone shot it."

"It's just cosmetic damage. I'll get it repaired when I'm back in Denver." She turned and moved into the living room, leaving him to close the door and follow.

"Who was shooting at you?" he asked. "Where were you? Why didn't you call and tell me?"

So much for keeping this from him. "I drove up to talk to Martin Kramer again," she said. "This morning. And I don't know who. The two of us were standing in front of his shack, talking, then someone started shooting at us."

"Are you all right?"

She supposed asking was a reflex, since he could clearly see she was fine. "Mr. Kramer and I are both unhurt," she said. "He shoved me under the car and started firing in the direction of the shots. I guess he scared off whoever it was."

"Did he have any idea who it was?" Shane asked.

"He said it was claim jumpers. You know he's convinced someone is trying to steal his gold mine. Though maybe there's something to that. He said various people have been harassing him since you and I were up there. At first, I thought maybe he was delusional, but I didn't imagine those gunshots."

"You shouldn't have gone up there by yourself," Shane said, as she had known he would. "You don't know anything about Kramer. He might have shot you himself."

"He didn't. In fact, he was very concerned for my safety." She had the skinned knees to prove it, from where he had shoved her down and urged her to hide under the car. "If you want to know more, you'll need to talk to him. So, you know what I did today. What did you do?"

"I finally talked to Anne-Marie Winstead Jones."

"Who?"

"Talia Larrivee's best friend. She didn't like Talia's new boyfriend, Tom, and thinks he probably killed her. She said Talia liked dangerous men."

"And Tom Chico is dangerous," she said. "Do you really think he murdered Talia?"

"I think right now he's our prime suspect. That doesn't mean we're not going to consider all the evidence, and everyone she came in contact with, but there's a good chance he was the last person she saw. And he seems to have disappeared."

"I asked Mr. Kramer if he thought Trey and Courtney and Tom were the people who have been harassing him recently," she said. "He said he didn't know. But maybe they are. Maybe he's right and they want his gold mine. We know they've been trying to get money other ways."

"I think I need to talk to Kramer again," he said. "And Sam Russell and the Olsens."

"I don't think I realized before how much investigations involve talking to people—sometimes the same ones over and over."

"When I started the job, the sheriff told me he thought I'd be good at it, because people like me and I'm easy to talk to. I thought he'd hired me because I was in shape and did well in my classes at the academy. He told me those things were important, but every department needed someone who was good at dealing with difficult people. He thought I could be their someone."

"And are you?" she asked. "Good at dealing with difficult people?"

"Pretty much." He flashed a smile. "Charm is my secret weapon."

She moved into his arms. "I guess I'm just another victim, then."

"Never a victim." He kissed her, his hand shaped to the curve of her hip.

"You never said why you stopped by tonight," she said.

"Because I wanted to see you. I wanted to do this." He kissed her again.

"This is nice," she said. "But I feel guilty that we're not doing more to find Courtney, or to locate Talia's killer."

"I had a professor in college who said that after a hard study session you should take a break for physical activity," he said. "While your body was exercising, your mind would sort out everything you had just learned and you could figure out any remaining problems. Something to do with oxygen flow to the brain and the activity or the subconscious and some other stuff I've forgotten."

"What kind of exercise?" she asked.

"When I was in college, I played ball or ran."

"Is that what you want to do now?" She nipped his neck.

"No. I'm thinking of another kind of exercise."

She let out a whoop as he scooped her into his arms and started toward the bedroom. She thought about telling him to put her down, but only briefly. She liked the feel of his strong arms around her. He wasn't physically dangerous, like the men Talia liked to hang out with. But there was something to be said for a little emotional risk in a relationship, shaking up the status quo and trying new things.

Like getting involved with a man she had fallen for hard. One she wasn't sure she'd ever figure out how to leave.

Chapter Seventeen

Fourth of July in Eagle Mountain was equal parts nostalgia and spectacle that not even a murder investigation could dim. The local scouting troop put out flags all along the town's main street, then a parade that included everything from the high school marching band to a dozen children on bicycles proceeded from the town hall to the town park. Shane and a few of the other deputies patrolled the crowd, alert for troublemakers, but this early in the day there were none.

After the parade, the craft booths and small carnival opened. The Rotary club sold barbecue dinners and the history museum staff handed out lemonade, and Saturday ended with a dance and fireworks. The festivities continued on Sunday, with a 5K run, a church service in the park and more barbecue. Sunday afternoon, Shane and his fellow deputies convened at the ball fields for the charity baseball game, which Adelaide delighted in telling everyone "raised more money this year than ever before."

Shane had told himself this was strictly amateur stuff, that he didn't care about the outcome and it didn't matter how he performed on the mound. But once he was up there in his uniform, clutching the ball and digging the toe of his cleat against the pitching rubber, he realized it mattered a great deal. In the eyes of everyone watching, he was still a pro ballplayer, and they expected a pro performance.

He struck out the first three batters he faced, and in the bottom of the inning Gage Walker hit a double off the fire department's pitcher. Travis followed that up with a solid single, allowing Gage to score, before Nate Hall struck out and Wes Landry hit a high fly ball. Another strikeout retired the side, but the sheriff's department was up one to nothing.

Shane struck out the next two batters, but the third player to face him that inning took advantage of a fastball he left hanging and hit the ball over the fence. The game was tied.

"He got lucky," Gage said when they returned to the dugout and prepared for their turn to bat. "It won't happen again."

"No, it won't," Shane said. He'd been taking it easy, trying not to show off too much, but he was done with that now. These people wanted a Major League show, he'd give them one.

After a series of singles and strikeouts by the sheriff's department players, it was Shane's turn to bat. He'd never been a hitter—it wasn't what they'd recruited him for and everyone knew it. He struck out, too. Then he was back on the mound, the crowd cheering wildly. He looked into the stands and spotted a couple of people wearing replicas of his pro jersey.

Then he saw Lauren, sitting next to Adelaide, a wide smile on her face, and he felt about ten feet tall. She didn't care how he pitched or whether he won or lost the game, but suddenly he wanted nothing more than to win—for her.

The firemen weren't pro ballplayers, but they weren't pushovers, easy. Shane walked a man, then the next got a weak single. But the next six in a row went down on strikes. And so it continued. By the time the seventh—and last—inning rolled around, someone had found a piece of chalk and scrolled a line of *K*s across the bottom of the outfield scoreboard—one for every strikeout Shane had thrown.

The score was three to one when Shane took the mound in the top of the seventh. There was no talk of anyone else pitching. Such a decision would have been met with derision from the crowd, some of whom were chanting his name as he exited the dugout. "Shane! Shane! Shane! Shane!"

He felt the soreness in his arm as he threw the first pitch. Not pain, just an awareness that he had thrown a lot today, and that it had been a long time since he'd worked his muscles this hard. But he had pitched much of his career with soreness, and he knew how to deal with that.

The first batter hit two foul balls before finally striking out. He walked the next man, who was short and stocky, and hunched over the plate, shrinking the strike zone, or so it seemed to Shane. The next man struck out and the fourth batter hit a single.

Shane hit the fifth batter. He wasn't aiming for the

guy, but he lost control of the ball and it thumped the man squarely on the shoulder. A groan rose from the crowd. The bases were now loaded.

"Come on, Shane!" someone yelled from the dugout. Gage, he thought.

Come on, Shane, he thought to himself, and rubbed up the ball. He tugged his hat down low and leaned toward the plate for the sign from the catcher. Not that Dwight was giving any signs. They had decided from the start that Shane would throw whatever Shane felt like throwing. Whatever the outcome of this game, it was all on him.

He wound up and threw. He winced at the sound of the ball connecting with the bat, and froze on the mound, afraid to turn around to see where the ball ended up. In the big leagues, a home run ball made a certain sound on the bat, a definitive crack like lightning striking. The metal bats they were using for this game had a different sound, loud and solid, but unreadable.

A cheer rose from the crowd and Shane forced himself to turn around. Nate stood near the outfield fence, the ball held triumphantly in his hand. Then some of the team was swarming Nate, while others gathered around Shane.

It wasn't the strikeout he would have scripted, but a fly ball was an out just the same. The sheriff's department had won the game and the cheesy trophy and bragging rights for the next year.

He searched the stands for Lauren, but she wasn't

there, her seat next to Adelaide vacant. Had she left the stands to meet him at the dugout?

He pushed through the crowd and made his way to the edge of the field. Adelaide leaned over the fence and raised her voice to be heard. "Great job out there!" she called.

"Thanks! Where's Lauren?"

Adelaide shrugged and shook her head.

He told himself not to worry—she'd probably just gone to the ladies' room, or had to take a call. He focused on accepting congratulations from those around him, then posing for a team photo with the trophy.

Thirty minutes had passed by the time he made it to the parking lot, and still no sign of Lauren. No one he spoke to had seen her. Fear took up residence in his chest, making it hard to take a deep breath. He texted her number and stared at the screen, willing her to reply. Nothing.

She had disappeared. And he had to find her.

As the sixth inning drew to a close, Lauren headed to the ladies' room. She joined the line of other women, some with children in tow, and made idle conversation about the weather and the game. She had never followed any sport, and had expected to be bored today. But she had found herself caught up in the game. Watching Shane on the mound was exciting, but listening to Adelaide's running commentary about the action on the field, she had found herself captured by the drama and strategy. There was a lot more going on out there than she had imagined.

She emerged from the restroom and gazed idly across the park. Children swarmed the playscape, scrambling up the climbing wall, soaring in the swings. Then a flash of blond hair made her heart stutter in its rhythm.

A little girl in a pink dress turned to call to another child, and Lauren gasped. "Ashlyn!" In her mind, she shouted the name, but it was really only a whisper. She scanned the group of adults around the playground. A blonde woman was half-hidden by a lamppost. Was that Courtney, in those oversize black sunglasses?

Lauren ran, darting around couples and family groups. She didn't care that people stared at her as she pushed past them. She reached the play area out of breath and had to stop a moment, half doubled over from a stitch in her side. She couldn't see the little girl anymore—Ashlyn. Or the woman she was now sure was Courtney.

She moved around the play area but couldn't find them. "Are you okay?" a woman asked, a young mother with a baby in a sling.

"Did you see a little girl in a pink dress, with long blond hair?" Lauren asked. "She was just here."

"No, I haven't." The woman put one hand protectively on the child in the sling. "Is she your little girl?"

"No, my niece. Her mother was with her, but I can't find them now."

The woman relaxed a little. "There are a lot of people here today. Maybe they went into the restroom."

There was a second set of restrooms near the playground. Lauren went inside, pushing past a line of women and children. "I'm just looking for someone," she said by way of apology. She stood outside the stalls and studied the feet of the people inside. "Courtney, are you in here?" she called. "Ashlyn, it's Aunt Lauren."

No one answered. Lauren went outside and waited a few minutes, watching people as they emerged from the restroom, but Courtney and Ashlyn weren't there.

Maybe they were in the parking area. Afraid she might already have missed them, she sprinted toward the paved lot behind the play area. Every slot was full, but she didn't see a blonde woman or little girl.

She returned to the play area, thinking maybe she had overlooked them. A dozen children swarmed the playscape and the adjacent array of oversize musical instruments, but no Ashlyn. No Courtney.

She didn't know how long she had been searching when Shane found her. He was still in his baseball uniform, worry making the lines around his gold-brown eyes deeper. "Lauren, what's going on?" he asked. "I've been looking for you."

The sight of him filled her with relief. "I saw Ashlyn," she said. "She was playing, right here." She gestured to the playscape. "And Courtney, too, I think. But by the time I ran over here, they were gone. I've been looking."

He put a hand on her shoulder. "Did you try calling Courtney, to let her know you were here?"

Why hadn't she thought of that? She pulled out her phone and sent a text. I'm here by the playscape. Please let me say hello to Ashlyn.

She waited, but there was no reply. "Give her a minute," Shane said.

She looked into his eyes, afraid of the doubt she might find there. "You believe me, don't you?" she asked. "You believe I saw them?"

"Yes."

She loved him in that moment, more than she already had. How many people would have tried to persuade her that she had merely seen someone who resembled her niece and her late brother's wife? Even if Shane was silently thinking that very thing, he didn't try to tell her so, and that counted for a lot.

"It's hot out here in the sun," he said. "Let's sit down in the shade."

He steered her toward the row of benches that moments before had been filled with people, but now there was room for the two of them on the end of one bench. "Great game, Shane," someone said as they passed.

"The game!" She forced her gaze from the playground area to look at him. "I'm sorry I left before the last inning. How did it go?"

He grinned, and the expression made him look boyish. "We won."

"It was exciting," she said. "I don't think I've ever sat and watched a whole game before. Well, almost a whole game. I liked watching you pitch."

"It was tougher than I thought it would be, being out there again." He rubbed his arm.

"Is your arm hurting?" she asked.

"Just a little sore." He laughed. "I'm out of shape."

Right. He was one of the fittest people she knew. She checked her phone again. "I don't think Courtney is going to reply," she said. "For some reason she's avoiding me."

"I'm sorry." He put his hand on her back. "I know how much you'd like to see her and your niece."

She nodded and searched through the crowd on the playground and around it again. "I don't think they're coming back," she said. "I guess we'd better go."

"We can stay as long as you like," he said.

He probably wanted to take a shower and get dinner. Her stomach growled, but she didn't think she'd be able to eat. "Let's go." She stood. She'd come to Eagle Mountain thinking Courtney and Ashlyn were the most important people in her life. Maybe that wasn't so true anymore.

MONDAY MORNING THE revelry of the day before was forgotten as the deputies and sheriff convened to discuss the murder investigation. Dwight had tracked a man he thought could be Tom Chico to a campsite in the national forest, but he had left the site a week before Talia's body was found.

Shane had submitted a written report on his interview with Anne-Marie Winstead Jones on Thursday, but the sheriff had him summarize it for the group now to refresh everyone's memory. "She said Talia told her she had an insurance policy she could use if Tom stepped out of line. Anne-Marie interpreted that as something Talia could hold over Tom and threaten to blackmail him with," he said.

"Like the photograph of Samantha Morrison," Travis said.

"That was the only reason Anne-Marie could think of for Talia to have that photograph," Shane said.

"Colorado Springs hasn't gotten back to me about any possible link between Morrison and Chico," Travis said. "I'll see if I can learn anything more when I talk to them today."

"I've been checking with hotels, motels and short-term rentals in a one-hundred-mile radius of Eagle Mountain," Jamie said. "No one has rented to anyone matching the descriptions of Tom Chico, Talia Larrivee, Courtney or Ashlyn Baker, or Trey Allerton. I would have thought someone would remember Courtney and Ashlyn in particular, but no luck so far."

"Lauren thought she saw Courtney and Ashlyn yesterday, at the playground next to the ball field," Shane said. He'd been debating whether or not to mention this. While he believed Lauren had seen someone who resembled her sister-in-law and niece, she couldn't be certain of their identity. "They left before she could speak to them."

"What about Allerton or Chico?" Gage asked.

"She didn't see them. And she only glimpsed the woman and the girl, though she's pretty certain of the ID."

Travis pointed a finger at Shane. "Remind Lauren she needs to come in and give a statement about what happened at the Full Moon Mine Wednesday," he said. "I stopped by Martin Kramer's place to talk to him. His truck was there, but I couldn't find him."

"Yes, sir," Shane said. He had reported Lauren's story of someone shooting at her and Kramer, and the sheriff had ordered him and Lauren to stay away from the mine. Instead, he'd had Shane looking for unsolved crimes similar to Talia's murder in every location Chico was known to have lived. There had been plenty of cases to consider, but nothing definitive.

A tap on the door made them all fall silent. "Come in," Travis called.

Adelaide stuck her head in the door. "There's someone here to see you, Sheriff," she said. Adelaide rarely let anyone in to see Travis without an appointment. If she was interrupting a meeting to let him know he was needed, the visitor must be someone important.

"Who is it?" Travis asked.

"He says his name is Trey Allerton. He heard you've been looking for him."

Chapter Eighteen

Trey Allerton strode into the interview room at the sheriff's office with the swagger of a closing pitcher who had just won the World Series. A tall, broad-shouldered man with a handsome, boyish face, he shook hands with both Travis and Shane, then dropped into the visitor's chair, perfectly at home. "I apologize I didn't get here sooner," he said. "I just heard you wanted to speak to me."

"Thank you for coming in," Travis said. "I've asked Deputy Ellis to sit in on this interview, which I'll be recording."

Allerton nodded to Shane. "I'm not sure what I can help you with," he said. "But I'll try."

Travis settled into the chair across from Allerton, while Shane stood to one side, against the wall. He had a good view of Allerton's face from here and was between him and the door. "When was the last time you saw Talia Larrivee?" Travis asked.

Allerton frowned. "Well, let me see. It's been a while, I guess."

Travis said nothing, waiting.

"I don't think I can give you an exact date," Allerton said. "Maybe a week or ten days ago? Tom brought her around one day to see the place we're leasing from Sam Russell. That's really why I'm in the county, you know. I'm going to start a camp for underprivileged youth up there. You know, get them in the outdoors, hiking and camping, maybe riding horses, really give them a new focus in life."

"What's your relationship with Tom Chico?" Travis asked.

The frown deepened, and Allerton shook his head. "Oh, Tom is a piece of work. He was going to partner with me on the youth camp project, but a little over a week ago, we had a falling out. I realized the two of us were never going to be able to work together, so we parted ways. All perfectly amicably, though I'm sorry I wasted so much time with him."

"Why weren't you going to be able to work with him?" Travis asked.

"Tom was a little bit of a loose cannon," Allerton said. "He had a temper. And he was impatient. I tried to explain to him that a project like this, if you're going to do it right, takes time. And money. He wanted to dive right in, start building and everything, but before we could do any of that, we had to raise money. A lot of it. I've been working on that, but not fast enough for Tom."

"How did the two of you meet?" Travis asked.

Allerton rubbed his jaw. "Let me see…" He brightened. "I remember now—Courtney introduced us."

"Courtney Baker?" Shane asked.

Allerton turned to look at him. "That's her. Sweet

girl. I think Tom went to her church. She said he was looking for work and I knew I'd need help with this ranch. Then he told me he had some savings he wanted to invest, and I figured why not?" He grimaced. "I guess that wasn't my best decision, though."

"Were you aware that Tom Chico had been in prison?" Travis asked.

Allerton nodded. "I found that out later, but like Courtney said, everybody deserves a second chance."

"When was the last time you saw Tom Chico?" Travis asked.

"Let me think." He sat back and crossed his ankle over one knee. "You have to realize I've been so busy, especially since Tom left, that it's hard to keep track." He tilted his head up and studied the ceiling. "I'd say it was right at a week to ten days ago. Can't be more specific than that—everything runs together. But Talia was with him. She'd been hanging around a lot lately." He chuckled. "Say what you will about Tom—I wouldn't have pegged him as a ladies' man, but Talia was crazy about him. And well, you know, she was a very good-looking woman. Rich, too. I really don't know how he did it."

"What was their relationship?" Travis asked.

"I never actually asked, but I'm pretty sure they were lovers."

"Would you say the two of them got along well?"

"Sure. Not that I saw them together that much, but she seemed really into him, and Tom liked her, too, I'm sure. I mean, she was young, rich, beautiful, and she appeared to adore him. What's not to like?"

"Where were you the last time you saw Tom Chico and Talia Larrivee together?" Travis asked.

"At the ranch. At the little trailer that's on the property. It was a dump when we first saw it, but we've fixed it up some and it will do until we get the financing to build something better."

"Who is we?"

"Me and Courtney. She's my other partner in this. The one I intend to keep. Her late husband was my best friend when I was in the army. The two of us got pretty close before he was killed in Afghanistan and we used to talk about opening a youth ranch somewhere in the Colorado mountains. Mike was killed over there, but after I got home, I visited Courtney, to pay my respects, you know. She and I really clicked. When I told her about the dream Mike and I shared, she was all for it. By then Mike had been gone two years and I think she was really lonely. And I was lonely, too. To tell you the truth, I was half in love with her before I ever met her. Mike used to talk about her all the time and I felt like I knew her."

"Where is Ms. Baker now?" Shane asked.

"Oh, she's back at the ranch. She's trying to lie low, you know, and avoid her annoying ex sister-in-law."

Shane stiffened. "What has her sister-in-law done that's annoying?" he asked.

"Oh, don't get me wrong." He sat up straighter, both feet flat on the floor. "It's great that Mike's sister is so loyal, but Courtney is a grown woman. She can look after herself and make her own decisions. Instead, Lauren thinks she has to run Courtney's life. No one wants to live like that."

"What about Ms. Baker's daughter, Ashlyn?" Shane asked.

"Sounds like you've been doing your homework," Allerton said. "Ashlyn is fine. She's with her mother."

"Back to Tom Chico," Travis said.

Allerton faced the sheriff once more. "I don't know what else I can tell you. We agreed to go our separate ways, and he and Talia left. I haven't heard a peep out of him since."

"Do you know where they were headed?" Travis asked.

"Nope."

Travis tapped a pen on his desk blotter. "Where was Chico staying?"

"I don't know that, either." Allerton leaned forward, elbows on the table, hands clasped. "Look, we were in business together, but we weren't really friends or anything. My focus has really been getting this ranch up and running."

"How much money did Chico contribute to the ranch?" Travis asked.

Allerton leaned back again. "That was a point of contention between us, too. He promised to pitch in twenty thousand dollars, but I never saw the money. He never came out and admitted he'd lied about having it, but I think that's what happened. Then he promised to get the cash, and the next thing I knew, he showed up with Talia on his arm. I think he thought he'd charm her into giving him the money. And the way she looked at him, he might have done it, too." He grinned. The look was probably meant to be boyish and charming. "Why all the questions about Talia and Tom?" he asked. "Has he done something wrong?"

"Ms. Larrivee's body was discovered several days ago in a remote area of the county," Travis said. "Mr. Chico may have been one of the last people to see her alive."

Allerton's charm deserted him, leaving him gaping and a little shrunken. "She's dead?"

"Ms. Larrivee was murdered," Travis said. "Do you have any information about that?"

Allerton held up both hands. "I don't have any information. I swear if I did, I'd tell you." He shook his head, as if trying to clear it. "Do you think Tom killed her?"

Travis didn't answer.

"Of course you think that," Allerton said. "It's why you asked me if they got along, and if I knew Tom had been in prison."

"Do you want to change anything about your earlier answers?" Travis asked.

"No. I told the truth—Tom and Talia seemed to get along great." He slumped in the chair. "But if you ask me if I think Tom *could* kill someone—maybe. I mean, he had a record, and he had a temper. If they did have a fight, maybe he knocked her around and she fell and hit her head?" He looked at the sheriff, as if for confirmation.

"Ms. Larrivee was shot," Travis said. "Did Chico own a gun?"

Allerton hesitated. "Mr. Allerton, did Tom Chico have a gun?" Travis asked again.

"I won't get in trouble, will I? I mean, ex-cons aren't supposed to have firearms, are they? And Tom did have a gun. I knew about it, but I didn't say anything because, well, because I'm smart enough not to start an argument with a man with a bad temper who has a gun."

"What kind of gun was it?" Travis asked.

"I don't know," Allerton said.

"How long were you in the army, Mr. Allerton?" Travis asked.

"Four years. And I get what you're saying. I ought to be familiar with guns, but I never saw this one out of the holster and I made a point of not looking at it too closely. I didn't want to know about it, you understand?"

"Is there anything else you can tell us about Tom Chico?" Travis asked.

"No. Except I'm sorry I ever met him."

"We'll need your contact information, in case we have more questions," Travis said.

"Sure, sure." He rattled off a phone number. "That's my mobile. There are a lot of places up here that don't have good coverage, but if I don't answer, leave a message and I'll get back to you, I promise."

"Deputy Ellis will show you out," Travis said.

Allerton didn't say anything as he and Shane walked down the hall to the front lobby. Shane thought the man beside him, shorn of his bravado and clearly shaken, was very different from the Trey Allerton they had first met.

Travis was emerging from the interview room when Shane returned. "Let's go into my office," the sheriff said.

Shane followed Travis into his office, which scarcely had room for the sheriff's desk, a bookcase and two visitors' chairs. The desk itself was neat, with only a laptop and one small stack of files, along with a photograph of Travis's wife, Lacy, mountains in the background.

"Impressions?" Travis asked as he settled behind the desk.

"He seemed genuinely shaken by the news that Talia was murdered," Shane said. "And maybe even afraid."

"Afraid of what we might find out?" Travis asked.

"Or afraid of Tom Chico. He might be thinking he's lucky he parted company with the man when he did."

"Or he could be lying about everything."

"He could," Shane agreed.

"What do you think of the story that Courtney Baker is avoiding Lauren?"

"Maybe she is. Lauren says she isn't trying to run Courtney's life, and I've never seen the two of them together to judge the relationship. But Lauren was very close to Courtney. She did Courtney's taxes and she says that Courtney is very naive and had been sheltered most of her life."

"I think she'd have to be naive to recommend Tom Chico as a business partner," Travis said.

"That was one part of Allerton's story that didn't ring true for me," Shane said. "I think he told us that because he doesn't want us to know the true circumstances of how he met Chico."

"Allerton doesn't have a record," Trey said. "As Trey Allerton or Troy Allen. But that could mean he just hasn't been caught yet. When I talk to Colorado Springs

PD, I'll ask about him, too. He was stationed in the area for a little while. Maybe he and Chico met up there."

"Do you think Courtney Baker and her daughter are safe with him?" Shane asked.

"We don't have any evidence that they aren't, but it wouldn't hurt to make sure. Why don't you swing by that trailer again and have a word with her?"

"I will." Maybe he would be able to reassure Lauren that Courtney and Ashlyn were all right and relieve a little bit of her worry.

LAUREN MADE IT a point to visit the shops nearest the sheriff's department midmorning, hoping she could catch Shane when he left the office to do whatever he was assigned to do that day. She could have called and asked him what the sheriff had to say about her sighting of Courtney and Ashlyn on Sunday, but it was always easier to talk face-to-face.

She almost didn't say anything when Shane emerged onto the sidewalk, telling herself she should be patient and wait until he was off duty that evening. Then he would probably call and tell her what she wanted to know. But just then he turned and spotted her. His smile filled her with warmth.

A few long strides brought him to her. "This is a nice surprise," he said. "What are you doing down here?"

"Hoping to see you," she said. "Sitting at home, not knowing what is going on was driving me to distraction."

"We've had some developments," he said.

"Anything you can tell me?"

"Walk with me, and we'll talk."

They headed down the sidewalk, the sparse crowd this time of day making it easy to walk side by side. He matched his stride to hers. "Trey Allerton stopped by the sheriff's department this morning," he said. "He said he heard we'd been looking for him."

She caught her breath. "Was Courtney with him?"

"No. But he assured us she and Ashlyn are fine."

She pressed her lips together to keep from saying she didn't trust anything Allerton said. But Shane already knew that. "What else did he have to say?" she asked.

"He was very cooperative and answered all our questions."

"He can be very charming. What did he have to say about Talia?"

"He said Tom Chico brought her to see the ranch and that she was very infatuated with him. Which is in line with what her best friend said about their relationship."

"Does Trey know where Tom is now?"

"He says he and Tom went their separate ways a week to ten days ago."

"Huh. Why is that?"

"He said it was because of Tom's temper, but I think the fact that Chico didn't come up with the money he was supposed to contribute to the youth ranch project might have had more to do with their parting of the ways."

"I told you Trey is more interested in money than anything else. It's why he went after Courtney."

"He said Courtney is the one who introduced him to

Tom. I'm glad I ran into you, because I wanted to ask you about that."

She stopped and faced him. "You're kidding! How would Courtney know an ex-con like Tom Chico?"

"Allerton said Tom attended her church and she was trying to help him out. Does that sound like something she would do?"

"Yes and no. I mean, Courtney does have a soft heart and she does try to help people. But she does things like babysit for a mom who has a job interview. Or she volunteers at the food pantry. She doesn't take ex-cons under her wing. And I'm positive she never mentioned anything like that to me."

"Maybe she didn't tell you because she knew it would upset you."

Maybe so. It seemed Courtney had kept other things from her, like the extent of her feelings for Trey Allerton. "I don't really care about Tom Chico," she said. "Did Trey say where Courtney and Ashlyn are?"

"He said they were waiting for him at the ranch. Supposedly, he's fixed up the trailer for the three of them to live in."

They started walking again. "I was just at the trailer on Wednesday," she said. "I stopped by on my way to see Martin Kramer. That place was in no shape to live in. And it was deserted."

She half expected him to be upset that she hadn't mentioned this until now, or to lecture her about going back out to the ranch after she had had a man pull a gun on her the last time she visited, but he didn't. "I'm going out there this afternoon to check out his story," he said. "I'm hoping to talk to Courtney."

She grabbed his arm. "Let me go with you. Please. If Courtney and Ashlyn are there, I need to see them."

He hesitated.

"What is it?" she asked, reading the distress on his face. "What's wrong?"

"Allerton said Courtney doesn't want to see you. He said she's avoiding you."

She released her hold on him. "That's a lie."

"You said when you spotted her and Ashlyn yesterday she left before you could speak to her."

"She has no reason to avoid me."

"She knows you don't approve of her relationship with Allerton. For some people, that would be enough."

She shook her head. How could she convince him that Courtney wasn't like that? The two of them had never openly argued about Allerton, and, while Lauren had tried to gently voice her concerns about Allerton, she had always acknowledged this was Courtney's decision to make. "I only want to make sure she's safe and happy," she said. "Take me with you to the ranch. If Courtney is there, you can see for yourself that she and I still have a good relationship."

"I'm going there to question a potential witness in a murder investigation," he said. "I can't take you with me."

"Fine. I'll drive out there myself." She fished her keys from her purse. "Now."

He reached for her hand. "No."

Tears stung her eyes. "Please," she said. "Take me

with you. I won't interfere with your work. But this is the whole reason I came to Eagle Mountain."

He squeezed her hand. "All right. But you need to stay in the cruiser until I'm sure it's safe."

"Of course."

They said little on the way out, but the silence wasn't uncomfortable. The low hum of the police radio provided a background for their few exchanges about the passing scenery and yesterday's game, the mundane topics providing momentary relief from the stress of this errand and everything behind it.

Shane slowed the cruiser as they neared the entrance to the Russell Ranch. "I want to stop in here a minute and see if Mr. Russell has heard or seen anything of interest," he said.

Mr. Russell was standing in front of the house when they pulled up, watching a younger man trim the branches of a large cottonwood. He walked over to them as Shane stopped the cruiser. "Hello, Deputy." He leaned down to look in the driver's window, which Shane had lowered, and nodded to Lauren. "Ma'am. What can I do for you today?"

"I wanted to check and see if you knew if anything was going on at that property you leased to Trey Allerton," Shane said.

"My hired man says they've been doing a little work around the place," Russell said. "They hired him to do a few odd jobs for them, but I don't know a lot else. They haven't bothered me any and I try to mind my own business."

"Have you spoken to anyone from there lately?" Shane asked.

"I haven't." The furrows on the old man's weathered face deepened. "They aren't mixed up in the murder of that girl, are they?"

"We don't know," Shane said. "We'd like to talk to Tom Chico, the older man, about that. If you see him around, will you call us? Don't try to talk to him yourself."

Russell nodded. "I will. I never liked the looks of that one. I should have listened to my instincts, I guess."

The door to the ranch house opened and a young woman with a long braid of dark hair stepped onto the porch. "Dad?" she called. "Is everything all right?"

"My daughter, Willow." Russell straightened. "Everything's fine," he said. He lowered his voice and spoke to Shane. "Don't say anything to her about all this. She worries me to death about living here by myself, even though it's not like I'm ever really alone, with all the hired help and all."

The woman watched from the porch, but made no move to join them. "I'll let you go now," Shane said. "We're going to drive on out to that property. Let us know if you see Tom Chico."

"I will," Russell said. "You take care, now."

"He's such a nice man," Lauren said as they pulled onto the road again. "I hope Trey and Tom leave him alone."

"I have a feeling he knows how to take care of himself," Shane said. "Most of these ranchers do."

The area around the battered trailer on Trey Allerton's lease looked as deserted as ever. Shane pulled into the drive, then turned so the cruiser was parallel to the trailer, pointed slightly toward the exit. He left the engine running and they both stared at the old mobile home. "Is this how it looked when you were here last week?" he asked.

"Yes. And the time before that. Although when I was here last, the door was locked."

He gave her a look that said he couldn't believe she tried to go inside, but said nothing. He cut the engine but left the keys in the ignition. "I'm going to go up and knock," he said.

She watched him as he approached the door, a big man with an easy, athletic gait. He undid the snap of his holster and kept close to the trailer as he climbed the steps, then knocked hard on the front door.

Lauren was sure the trailer was empty, but after only a few seconds, the door eased open. Courtney stood in the open doorway, lovely as ever. The relief that flooded Lauren propelled her out of the car before she even registered what was happening. Shane turned and said something to her, but she was too focused on Courtney to acknowledge anything else. "Thank God you're all right," she said.

"Hello, Lauren," Courtney said. She wasn't smiling, but she didn't look angry, either. Courtney took a step back and held the door open wider. "Deputy Ellis was telling me he has a few questions. You might as well come in."

Chapter Nineteen

Shane could have berated Lauren for ignoring his order to stay in the car, but he decided to save his breath. Once inside the trailer, the two women embraced, and the affection between them seemed genuine. He had a good view of Courtney's face from where he stood by the door, and he would have said the expression reflected there was relief, as if some burden had been lifted.

At last they parted, though Lauren kept hold of Courtney's hand. Then a little blonde girl, barefoot and wearing a pink sundress, long blond curls tumbled around a cherubic face, raced into the room and launched herself at Lauren, who scooped her up, laughing. "Ashlyn, look at you!" Lauren declared. She hugged the child, then looked at Ashlyn. "I heard she'd been sick and I was worried."

Courtney looked surprised. "How did you hear that?"

"It doesn't matter. She's okay now, right?"

"Of course. It was just a little stomach virus. She's loving it here in the country." She stroked her daughter's curls as she spoke. "My little wild child."

Lauren balanced Ashlyn on one hip and looked

around the table. "How long have you been living here?" she asked.

"Just a couple of nights," Courtney said. "It's only temporary, until we can build a better place to live, but I don't need anything fancy. Come on and sit down."

The two women and the girl sat on a worn plaid sofa while Shane took the only other seat in the room—a metal folding chair. "Where were you before you moved here?" Lauren asked. "Why didn't you return my calls and texts?"

"We were moving around a lot," Courtney said. "I kept meaning to answer you, but we were so busy." She shrugged. "The time never seemed right." She turned to Shane. "What did you want to ask me about, Deputy?"

Hurt shone in Lauren's eyes. Shane forced his attention away from her. He had a job he needed to do. "Trey Allerton stopped by the sheriff's department this morning to answer some questions," Shane said.

"Yes, he mentioned he was going to do that," Courtney said.

Lauren looked around the room again. Someone had cleaned the place since Shane had last seen it. "Where is Trey now?" Lauren asked.

"He had some errands to run," Courtney said. "I don't expect him for a while."

"I'd like to ask you some questions, also," Shane said. "The sheriff's department is investigating the murder of Talia Larrivee, and you may have been one of the last people to see her alive."

"Ashlyn, honey, you need to go play in your room now," Courtney said.

"But I want to stay with Aunt Lauren!"

"I'll go play with you," Lauren said. She stood. "I want to see your room."

Shane sent her a grateful look, then turned back to Courtney. She was a small woman, with delicate features, porcelain skin and very clear blue eyes. "Lauren has been very worried about you," he said, after Lauren and Ashlyn had left the room.

"I know." Courtney tucked a strand of her long blond hair behind one ear. "Maybe it's the nurse in her. She feels she has to look after people. But Ashlyn and I are fine, really."

"You don't seem shocked to hear that Talia is dead," he said.

"Murder is a horrible thing," she said. "A shocking thing. But we heard the news a couple of days ago."

"How did you hear?" Shane asked.

"Trey brought home a newspaper with the story."

So Allerton had been faking his shock in the sheriff's office. "Was Talia comfortable with Tom? Was she afraid of him?"

"I don't think she was afraid of anything." She shook her head. "I didn't really like her. Is that horrible to say about someone who is dead now? But it's the truth. I thought she was too wild and vulgar. She was always kissing Tom and draping herself over him, and at least once when they were here, I'm sure they had both been drinking. It's not the kind of behavior I want Ashlyn to see. I told Trey so and he promised to speak to them."

Laughter sounded from down the hall. Courtney looked in that direction and smiled. "Ashlyn has really missed her aunt," she said. "Thank you for bringing Lauren here today."

"Trey Allerton said you've been avoiding Lauren—that you resent the way she's interfered in your life."

Pain flickered in her blue eyes. "Trey resents what he sees as Lauren's interference. I know Lauren is just concerned for my safety."

"But you do seem to have been avoiding her. She said you saw her at the playscape yesterday and you left before she could reach you. And I have to think if you'd really wanted to return her texts or calls, you'd have found the time to do so."

She smoothed her hands down her thighs. "Sometimes it is easier to stay away than to deal with the conflict. I'm not proud of that, but it's true."

"Conflict with Lauren?"

"And with Trey. He would rather I didn't see her."

"Is he trying to keep you from your family and friends?" Shane asked. That kind of controlling behavior could be a sign of an abusive relationship.

"Of course not," she said. "He just says—and I agree—that while we're involved in getting this project off the ground, we don't need distractions. And I know Lauren is disappointed in me. I hate that, so I guess I'm being a coward and trying to avoid confrontation, with her and with Trey." She shrugged. "It's not an ideal situation, but Ashlyn and I are fine, I promise. And when this ranch opens for the children, it will all be worth it."

"Where were you between the time you left the Ranch Motel and moving here?" he asked. She had blown off Lauren with a vague answer, but he wouldn't let her get away with that with him.

"We stayed in a rental cabin outside of Telluride for a week," she said, "then a couple of different motel rooms in Rico and Dolores. We were waiting for this place to be ready." She looked around the trailer. "I know to a lot of people this seems like a step down from where we used to live, but material things aren't important to me. Making this ranch a reality and helping those children is."

"Tell me about the ranch," Shane said. He had heard Lauren's and Allerton's versions of the story, but he was curious to know Courtney's view of the project.

"It's an idea Trey and my late husband, Mike, came up with over in Afghanistan," she said. "Planning it was a way to distract themselves from everything over there. It will be a beautiful retreat in the mountains where children from the inner city or those who have suffered trauma can come and relax and spend time in nature. We'll have horses and a pond where they can fish, trails they can hike and activities like archery and climbing. We'll have trained counsellors who can help the children. It's going to be really beautiful."

Her expression grew dreamy as she spoke, as if she was no longer seeing the dingy trailer but the camp that was to be. "It takes a lot of money to build something like that," he said.

She shrugged. "I have a lot of money. Or rather, it was Mike's money. I want to use it to create something he would be proud of."

"My understanding is much of that money is in a trust," Shane said.

She sighed. "Yes. Which makes it difficult. But Trey is working hard to get the additional funds we need."

"What is he doing to get the money?" Shane asked.

"You'd have to ask him. I'm not involved in that part of it."

"You sent a text to Lauren that upset her," Shane said. "She said it was a message for help because you referred to your late husband as Michael and yourself as Court—names you don't normally use."

Her expression clouded. "I never should have sent that message," she said. "I was upset that day."

"What were you upset about?"

She cupped her hands around her knees. "Tom was here, and he and Trey were arguing. I was afraid. But then he left and things got better."

"When did Tom leave?"

She pursed her lips. "A week ago? A little more? He and Trey had a big fight, about money, I think. Tom was supposed to contribute money to the project and he didn't."

"Was Talia Larrivee with Tom that day?"

"Yes. She was always with Tom the last week or so that he was here."

Shane took a card from his pocket and passed it to her. "If you ever need anything, anything at all, call me."

She looked at the card, then slipped it into her pocket. "That's very kind of you, but I'm sure it won't be necessary." She met his gaze with a steady look of her own.

"Lauren thinks I'm fragile and naive because that's the woman Mike married. But I've been on my own for a while now—when Mike was deployed, and after he died. I've grown up a lot. I still tend to believe the best in people, but that's not the same as being ignorant of how badly they can behave." She stood. "I'm sure you have things to do, so let's go get Lauren."

Lauren and Ashlyn were seated on the floor of the first small room on the left side of the hallway, a collection of dolls with brightly colored hair spread out between them. Lauren was braiding the hair of a doll with pink hair, while Ashlyn combed the purple mane of another. "It's time for Aunt Lauren to go now," Courtney said. "You need to say goodbye."

"But I don't want her to go," Ashlyn said.

Lauren looked from Shane to Courtney, then stood. "I'll come back and play with you again soon," she said. "If that's all right with your mother."

"Of course," Courtney said. "We could even come see you."

"I hope you will come see me." Lauren put both hands on Courtney's shoulders. "You're really okay out here by yourself?" she asked.

Courtney nodded. "I'm fine. I was upset when Tom was here. I was telling Deputy Ellis that's why I sent that weird text message. But everything is fine now. I know Trey isn't your favorite person, but he and I are working hard to make this youth ranch a reality." She smiled, an expression that transformed her face from merely pretty to gorgeous. "I haven't been this excited about anything in a long time. This is going to be something that would really make Mike proud. We're going to name it after him, did I tell you that?"

Lauren shook her head. Unlike her sister-in-law, she looked stricken. She swallowed hard and forced a smile that didn't reach her eyes. "Call me if you need anything," she said. "And stay in touch."

"I will. It's hard, since cell service is so lousy up here. But I'll do my best." She patted Lauren's shoulder. "And don't worry. I really am fine."

Lauren remained silent as they returned to the car. At the road, Shane headed right. "I want to revisit the crime scene," he said. "Will you be all right waiting in the car?"

She nodded. He searched for something to say that might comfort her. "Courtney looked good. She seems to know what she's doing."

"It still worries me, her and Ashlyn up here alone with that man. And I hate that Trey has made her believe that this ranch is something Mike wanted." She drew a deep breath and sat up straighter. "But she's a grown woman. She has the right to make her own decisions. And I guess I do feel better, knowing Tom Chico isn't around anymore. At least Trey made the right decision, getting rid of him."

"They seem very serious about this ranch idea."

"Courtney is serious. I'm still suspicious of Trey, but I guess I'll just have to wait and see."

He wanted to ask her if she intended to return to Denver now that she had spoken to Courtney and seen for herself that she and Ashlyn were okay. His hands tightened on the steering wheel. He wasn't ready to hear

her answer. Sure, people could have long-distance relationships, and Denver was only a six-hour drive away,
but it wouldn't be the same as having her here all the
time, spending every night together, as they had fallen
into the habit of doing.

Yellow crime scene tape fluttered from a bush, marking the trail up to the ruined cabin where Talia's body
had been found. Shane parked the cruiser in the shade
of a gnarled pinion, lowered the windows and shut off
the engine. "It will take a while to hike there and back,"
he said.

"I'll be fine." She looked out the window. "If you
didn't know what had happened up here, this would be
a very peaceful spot." She glanced back at him. "Are
you looking for something in particular?"

He shook his head. "I just want to see it again, and
think about how it may have played out. Refresh the details in my mind." It probably wouldn't help them find
Tom Chico, but he thought it might help him cement
his focus on solving the crime. All of the drama with
Allerton and Courtney, and even Lauren, was outside
of that. He needed to think about Talia, and Tom, who
was looking more and more like the murderer.

AFTER SHANE HAD disappeared from sight down the trail,
Lauren gazed out at the silent landscape and tried to let
the peace of the scenery fill her. She had seen Courtney
and Ashlyn. They were both safe and seemingly con-
tent with the new life they had chosen. She had done
what she came to Eagle Mountain to accomplish, so
she should be happy.

But today had felt like another loss in the string of losses since Mike had died. It was good to see Courtney not as weighed down with grief as she had been. The youth ranch project had given her a new focus in life. She had a new strength Lauren hadn't seen before.

But there had been a new distance between her and Lauren also. Courtney had a different life now, and the two women would never be as connected as they once were. Lauren would learn to accept this, but for now she allowed herself to mourn a little.

"I did what I could, Mike," she whispered. "I looked after her as long as she needed me to, but I think she's ready to move on." Lauren would have to move on, too.

It was warm in the car, even in the shade. She pushed open the door and let the breeze wash over her, then stood and stretched. She'd been in Eagle Mountain two weeks and hadn't ventured very far into these beautiful mountains. She should ask Shane to take her hiking. Not here, but some other trail.

Something stirred behind her and she turned, expecting to see Shane heading up the trail toward her. Instead, an older man stood beside the sheriff's department cruiser—dark haired, olive complected, with a network of black tattoos up both arms and a jagged fresh cut across his right cheek. Tom Chico.

She stood a step back. "What do you want?" she asked.

His gaze slid over her, then across the cruiser and back. Before she could react, he strode forward and seized her by the arm. "Right now, I want you."

AN HOUR AFTER leaving Lauren, Shane completed his review of the crime scene and headed back toward the trailhead at a brisk walk. He was almost to the parking area when he stopped, struck by the stillness around him. The passenger door of his cruiser stood open, and from here the vehicle appeared empty. "Lauren!" he called.

No answer.

Then he was running to the empty cruiser. "Lauren!" he called again, looking around him. Heart pounding, he looked first one way, then the other, for any sign of her. Had she slipped into the underbrush to relieve herself? Had she decided to walk back down the road to visit Courtney again?

He shook his head. The trailer where Courtney and Ashlyn lived was several miles from here. And if Lauren had gone to relieve herself, she wouldn't have gone so far that she couldn't hear him calling her.

Think! he told himself. *Think like a cop.*

He studied the area around the car, but the red gravel revealed no footprints or signs of a struggle. The surface was too hard to show the imprints of tires. Finally he gave up. He wasn't getting anywhere with this scrutiny. He tried to key the radio but was rewarded only with static. The department's repeater system was unreliable, and the county budget had yet to find funds to add more towers. He'd have to drive until he got a signal, then call for help.

He drove as fast as he dared on the rough road, sliding around turns, gravel flying up behind him. He turned in at the entrance to the Full Moon Mine. Martin Kramer was sifting through a mound of rock by his shack and looked up when Shane's cruiser skidded to a halt beside him. "I'm looking for Lauren Baker, the woman who visited you the other day, when someone fired on the two of you," Shane said, the words coming out in a rush.

"I haven't seen her," Kramer said.

"Have you seen anyone else today?" Shane asked. "Anyone at all?"

"No. For once it's been quiet around here."

"If you see Lauren, go to a neighbor's and call 911," he said. Not waiting for an answer, he left.

He went on to the trailer. Courtney came out to meet him. "Lauren is missing," he told her. "I left her in the car while I checked on the crime scene up at the Sanford Mine, and when I returned, she was gone. Have you seen her or heard from her?"

"No." Courtney shook her head, her fair skin even paler. "I don't understand. Do you think she walked away?"

"Do you think she would do that?"

"No." Another shake of the head.

"I'm worried someone took her." He got back in the cruiser. "If you see or hear from her, call me."

No one was at the Olsens' yurt. Shane called for Lauren and looked for any sign she had been there but came up empty.

At last Shane turned in at the Russell Ranch. When Willow Russell answered the front door, Shane asked, "Do you have a landline phone? Can I use it?"

"Of course." She opened the door wider to let him in.

"What's wrong?" Samuel Russell asked when Shane followed Willow into the living room. Sam sat in a recliner, a small terrier on his lap.

Shane didn't answer but dialed the sheriff's direct number. When Travis answered, Shane had to force the words out. "Lauren is missing," he said. "We were up at the crime scene. I left her alone for a few moments, and when I came back, she was gone."

He had left her and she was gone. He prayed that knowledge didn't haunt him for the rest of his life.

Tom Chico smelled like sweat and woodsmoke. The bandana he had shoved into Lauren's mouth when she started to scream tasted like dirt. She couldn't think about it or she'd gag. His fingers dug into her arm as he dragged her alongside him, hurting her. She believed he wanted to hurt her. Is this what Talia had felt in the moments before he shot her?

She pushed that thought away, too. She couldn't give in to terror. She needed to pay attention to her surroundings, to figure out where he was taking her. But nothing in this landscape looked familiar. They moved through groves of evergreen trees, over red and gray rock, with occasional glimpses of blue sky and green valleys. They climbed for a while, breathing hard in the high altitude, and once they crossed a small stream, the water red-orange from minerals in the soil. They weren't following any trail that she could discern, but he seemed to know where he was going. Whenever she could, she made a point of brushing against trees or dragging her

feet in the dirt, hoping to provide a trail others could
follow.

She didn't know how long they had been walking
before he stopped, but she thought it was over an hour.
He shoved her ahead of him into a thicket of deep brush.
She tried to shield her face with her hands, but thorns
raked across her, tearing her flesh and catching at her
clothing.

And then she was free of the underbrush, standing
in a small circular clearing with a rock firepit in the
center and a green nylon dome tent erected at one side.

Tom pulled the bandana from her mouth. "Scream
all you want," he said. "No one will hear you out here."

"What do you want with me?" she asked, afraid of
the answer but needing to know.

"I need you to get past the cops that are looking for
me." He sat on the ground in front of the tent and motioned for her to do the same. "You might as well take
a load off," he said. "I imagine it will take a while for
them to find us."

She looked past him at the wall of underbrush around
them. Could she break through there and run back the
way they came? "If you try to run, I'll shoot you," he
said, and opened his jacket to show a pistol in a holster
at his belt. "Better to wait."

"Wait for what?" She sat as far from him as she
could get in the small clearing, her back against the
trunk of a tree.

"That cop you were with and his friends will track
us here eventually," he said. "Then we'll make a deal."

She wanted to keep him talking. As long as he was

talking, he wasn't doing something to hurt her. "How did you get way out here?" she asked. "I never saw a car."

"I got as far as I could, then hit a rock and tore a hole in the oil pan. I shoved the wreck over a cliff so no one would spot it and I made it back here on foot." He looked around. "I like to camp, figured I would hole up here awhile, then maybe I'd run off that old miner up the road and move into his place. Then I saw you and came up with a different plan."

"What happened to Talia?" she asked. She braced herself, half expecting the question to enrage him.

"Talia did something stupid," he said, his voice as calm as if he had said that Talia had bought grapes at the grocery store. "She thought her money protected her. Sometimes it does, but not this time."

"I thought you and Trey Allerton were partners. You were going to open a youth ranch together."

"Right. It was a good cover story, anyway. Trey told me we'd make a ton of money with that scam, but he wasn't coming across with the cash, so I moved on." He shrugged. "He and that woman he's with—Courtney—are both dumb, but Trey is dangerous because he thinks he's smart."

"Trey told the sheriff that Courtney introduced the two of you—that you went to her church."

He smirked. "I've known Trey a long time. Way before she showed up. But he probably thinks that story sounds better. He's a born con artist. He's good at figuring out what people want to hear and giving it to them."

This confirmation of her worst fears about Trey

made her stomach hurt. "What kind of deal are you hoping to make with the sheriff?" she asked.

"I guess we'll find out, won't we?" He grinned, a look that sent ice through her. It was the look of a man who saw her not as a person but as a commodity he could bargain with—and one he could discard without a second thought if she was no longer useful to him.

She couldn't give in to fear. Shane would be looking for her. When he got back to the cruiser and she wasn't there, he would start a search. She and Tom were on foot, just the two of them. Shane would have the whole sheriff's department—the whole town—helping to look for her.

All she had to do was stay alive long enough for him to find her.

Chapter Twenty

Shane reminded himself that as much as he wanted to charge off across the mountains in search of Lauren, floundering around with no idea of what direction to take could destroy potential evidence, and even endanger his own life or Lauren's. So he forced himself to wait the long forty-five minutes it took for Travis and Gage Walker to arrive at the trailhead.

Shane went over everything again—how he had visited the crime scene and found no new insight, then returned to the cruiser, where he had left Lauren. "The passenger door was open and she was gone," he said. "No one else was around. Lauren didn't answer my calls." The sheriff didn't ask why Shane had brought a civilian with him to question a witness, or berate him for doing so. "Let's get a search dog up here," he said. "Gage, see if Lorna Munroe from Search and Rescue is available. If we can get an idea which direction Lauren headed from here, we can focus our search better."

Other deputies arrived, and they spent the next hour combing the area immediately around the parking lot. They found an empty water bottle, a shoelace, a candy wrapper and a strip of survey ribbon—nothing connected to Lauren, but it was all dutifully catalogued. Gage returned to report that Lorna Munroe and her search dog, Daisy, were on their way.

"What do you think happened?" Gage asked, though Shane wasn't sure if the question was addressed to him or the sheriff.

"Random abductions happen," Travis said. "But given the remote location, that seems unlikely."

"Who would be hanging around a crime scene?" Gage asked.

"The murderer." Shane hadn't meant to say the word out loud, but no one reacted in shock or tried to deny the possibility. "Tom Chico has to know we're looking for him," Shane continued. "He's our chief suspect for the murder of Talia Larrivee. He may have murdered Samantha Morrison." He gritted his teeth, unable to carry the thought any further. If a man like that had Lauren...

Travis clamped a hand on his shoulder. "Do you want to go back to town?" he asked.

"No!" He didn't want to leave here until Lauren was found.

"Then get with Dwight and climb that peak over there and see if you can make out anything that will help us." He pointed to a high point a half mile away.

It was busy work. Something to keep Shane's body, if not his mind, occupied. But he appreciated it and set out with Dwight to climb the peak, where they had a view of the surrounding landscape, and realized how difficult it was to make out anything in the dense groves of trees and scattered boulders.

When they returned over an hour later, more cars filled the lot. "When Lorna and her dog return from their survey of the area, we'll start the search," Travis said. "She should be able to give us an idea of the best direction to cover. Groups of four, everyone armed and alert. No civilians this first pass, since we don't know what we're going to find. Shane, you come with me, Dwight and Jamie. Gage, stay here to coordinate the scene."

They turned at the sound of someone approaching. A large brown dog with long legs and drooping ears burst from the woods and trotted toward them, tongue lolling. A petite middle-aged woman with short-cropped blond hair followed soon after, trailed by Deputy Wes Landry. "There's a good strong trail through there," she said, indicating a northeasterly direction. "Daisy isn't having any trouble following it. It's so good I made her turn around so we could get you. I didn't want to come up on trouble by myself."

"Are you okay leading us in, Lorna?" Travis asked. "We don't know what we're going to find here. I'll ask you to back off if there's any hint of trouble, but I can't guarantee you won't get involved if it gets ugly."

"I'm trained for this kind of thing," she said. She looked over her shoulder, in the direction she had just come. "It was a good trail. I think we can find her."

They set off, Lorna and her dog in front with the sheriff, Shane bringing up the rear. They moved quickly, the dog running ahead, then stopping to wait for them. "Can you tell if she's following one or two people?" Dwight asked.

"No way to tell," Lorna said. "She's been told to track Lauren, so she's homing in on the scent on that purse and water bottle Travis showed us. But if there's someone with her, the dog may follow that scent, too, especially if it's stronger."

"But you're sure she's still following Lauren's scent?" Travis asked.

"She's an experienced tracking dog," Lorna said. "She might lose a weak scent, but I've never known her to follow a false trail."

"Hey, I've got something here," Jamie called. They all turned toward her, and she pointed to a bush beside the trail. "There's a thread of blue fabric here."

Shane moved in beside her and stared at the thread caught on a twig. "Lauren is wearing a shirt that color," he said.

"Flag it," Travis said. "If we need to, we can come back to it later."

They continued following the dog, in no way quiet or stealthy. Jamie dropped back to walk nearer Shane. "The sheriff must be expecting trouble, to bring us all along," she said.

"I was thinking the same thing," Shane said.

"If someone did take Lauren, it was probably only one person," she said. "We'll have the advantage in numbers."

After about an hour of walking, Daisy stopped and sat. "What's she doing?" Dwight asked.

"She's gone as far as she can go," Lorna said. She took a treat from the pouch at her waist and fed it to the dog.

Travis looked around at the thick underbrush. "Do you mean she's lost the scent?"

"She hasn't lost it," Lorna said. "This is as far as she can go." She brushed one hand across the greenery in front of them. "These wild roses are too thick for her to get through."

"I think someone has been through them." Jamie indicated a broken branch. "Not too long ago, either."

Then a woman's scream rent the air, high and long, and terrifying.

ONE MOMENT, Lauren was seated on the ground, trying not to think about the rock digging into her backside and wondering how Tom would take it if she got up and walked around, the next he had grabbed her, jerked her to her feet and pressed a knife to her throat. "Scream!" he commanded.

Stunned, she didn't comply right away. He pressed the tip of the knife into her flesh, and startled, she yelped.

"You'll have to do better than that." He pressed the knife deeper. A hot sting, then a wet trickle down the side of her neck.

She screamed, loud and long until her throat was raw. There was a commotion on the other side of the bushes, then they split apart and Shane, followed by the sheriff and two other officers, stepped into the clearing.

The knife bit again, and Tom's arm around her tightened until she could scarcely breathe. "Don't come any closer," he said. "I swear I'll cut her."

Through a film of tears, Lauren watched Shane. She had never seen a man look so angry.

"Let her go, Tom," the sheriff said. "We'll talk about this."

"I'll do the talking," Tom said.

"I'm listening," Travis said.

"All of you, stand out here where I can see you." Tom shifted and drew the gun.

Lauren watched him out of the corners of her eyes. Her knees had turned to jelly and she fought to keep her breathing even. *You have to be strong*, she told herself. *If you have a chance to get away, you can't blow it.*

The deputies did as he asked, arranging themselves on either side of the sheriff in a line.

"Throw out your weapons. There, by the fire." Tom gestured with the gun.

Slowly, with careful movements, each officer removed his or her gun from the holster and slid it toward the firepit. Lauren tried not to look at Shane, but her gaze kept drifting back to him. Every time, she found his eyes fixed on her. That steady look comforted her, even as she worried it made him more vulnerable. What if Tom did something to hurt him and Shane didn't see the threat because he was focused on her?

"I'm going to tell you what I want, then you're going to leave here and get it for me," Tom said. "She—" he shook Lauren "—stays here until I get everything. And I mean everything."

Travis remained silent, and his face betrayed nothing, his jaw set, eyes hard.

"I want a helicopter up here, twenty thousand dollars in unmarked bills, in a backpack," Tom said. "I want the chopper to take me to Ciudad Juárez."

"Is that it?" Travis asked after a long moment of silence.

"I can make it more complicated if you like," Tom said.

"Did you kill Talia Larrivee?" Travis asked.

"I'm not answering any questions." Tom tightened his hold on Lauren again. "Get out of here now. You've got work to do."

"Let her go." Shane took a step forward. "I'll stay instead."

"The star pitcher," Tom said. "What am I going to do with you?" He shook his head. "Get out of here."

When they didn't move, he raised the pistol—not aimed at Lauren, but at Shane, an easy target standing in front of the others. Lauren's vision blurred as she imagined a bullet slamming into Shane. She screamed and doubled over. The gun fired, the report echoing around them. More shots were fired and in the chaos someone shouted for her to get down.

She didn't need the reminder. She was on her stomach, crawling toward the edge of the clearing. And then Shane was with her, his body covering hers even as the clearing around them fell silent.

"I'm okay," she reassured him. "Please tell me you're okay, too."

"I'm fine." He pulled her tight against him, against the hard wall of his ballistics vest. She stared at him, examining his face to make sure he was telling the truth.

"He was aiming right at you," she said.

"And you threw off his aim when you ducked. It was enough time for me to dive to the ground."

She looked over his shoulder, at Tom Chico lying on the ground, blood pooling around him. "Is he dead?" she asked.

"I think so, yeah." He lifted her chin and frowned. "You're bleeding where he cut you."

She touched her hand to the sticky warmth along the side of her neck. "It's not very deep," she said. "I'll be okay." Though it might be a while before she could close her eyes and not feel the terror she had felt with that knife pressed to her throat.

Shane helped her to her feet but kept a tight hold on her as they moved toward the sheriff, who stood to one side, surveying the camp. "We know he was camping out in another part of the county for a while," he said. "He must have moved here sometime after that."

"He said he busted the oil pan on his car when he hit a rock and he pushed the wrecked vehicle over a cliff," Lauren said. "He said he hiked in from there. He said something about staying here until he could run Martin Kramer off his claim, but then he saw me and came up with a different plan."

Voices rose behind them, then the underbrush parted and Gage and the rest of the force pushed in, a slight woman with a dog bringing up the rear. "I ran all the way back to the parking area," she told Travis. "I've never run so fast in my life."

The sheriff put his arm around the woman's shoulders and hugged her. "You deserve a medal, Lorna," he said. "Thanks for everything."

"Is everyone okay?" Lorna looked around the clearing, then her gaze rested on Tom Chico and her face lost most of its color.

"You go on back with Shane and Lauren," Travis said, turning her away. "I'll take care of things here."

No one said much of anything until they were back at the parking area. Lorna had regained her color by then and reassured them she was okay to drive herself home. She loaded the dog into her SUV and set out.

"I should take you to the hospital," Shane said.

Lauren bent and examined her neck in the side mirror of his cruiser. "I don't need a hospital," she said. "I can clean and dress this myself at home."

"I guess you could." He looked dazed still, so she put her arms around him and hugged him close. "The four of you saved my life," she said. "But I knew you'd come for me. I'm just glad you weren't hurt."

"I've never felt as terrible as I did when I had to stand there and watch him cut you," he said. "Enraged and helpless and…"

"Shhh." She pressed the tips of her fingers to her mouth. "It's okay. It's all over now."

"It's not over." He pulled back, just far enough to meet her gaze. "I would have done anything to save you in that moment. That's how much you've come to mean to me. I love you, Lauren."

Something expanded in her chest, something that felt almost too big to contain. "I love you, too," she said.

"Are you going back to Denver?" he asked. "I know your job and your home and probably your whole life is there, so it's okay if you do, as long as I can come with you."

"I think my life is here now," she said. "You're here, but so are Courtney and Ashlyn. They're the only family I have left, so I'd like to stay close, just in case they need me."

"What about your job?"

"The clinic here offered me a job, remember? And Eagle Mountain is really growing on me. I think I'm going to like it here."

"Enough to get married?" He held up a hand. "I'm not trying to rush you, but when you're ready, I'd really like us to be husband and wife."

It wasn't a grand romantic declaration or a poetic promise, but the sincerity of his plea, and his concern for her feelings, melted her heart. "Yes, I'll marry you," she said, and kissed him with all the passion the moment called for. She'd made mistakes before, falling too hard and fast. But this time, she'd gotten it right. When she'd looked into Shane's eyes in Tom Chico's camp, her heart had known this was the man for her. And she was the right woman for him.

* * * * *

*Look for the next book in
Cindi Myers's
Eagle Mountain: Search for Suspects
on sale in February 2022!*

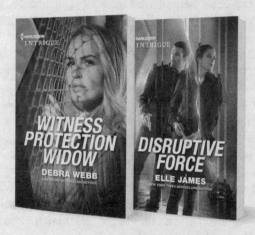

#2049 MURDER ON PRESCOTT MOUNTAIN
A Tennessee Cold Case Story by Lena Diaz

Former soldier Grayson Prescott started his cold case firm to bring murderers to justice—specifically the one who destroyed his life. When his obsession intersects with Detective Willow McCray's serial killer investigation, they join forces to stop the mounting danger. Catching the River Road rapist will save the victims...but will it save their future together?

#2050 CONSPIRACY IN THE ROCKIES
Eagle Mountain: Search for Suspects • by Cindi Myers

The grisly death of a prominent rancher stuns a Colorado community and plunges Deputy Chris Delray into a murder investigation. He teams up with Willow Russell, the victim's fiery daughter, to discover her father's enemies. But when Willow becomes a target, Chris suspects her conspiracy theory might be right—and larger than they ever imagined...

#2051 GRAVE DANGER
Defenders of Battle Mountain • by Nichole Severn

When a young woman is discovered buried alive, Colorado ME Dr. Chloe Pascale knows that the relentless serial killer she barely escaped has found her. To stop him, she must trust police chief Weston Ford with her darkest secrets. But getting too close is putting their guarded hearts at risk—and leading into an inescapable trap...

#2052 AN OPERATIVE'S LAST STAND
Fugitive Heroes: Topaz Unit • by Juno Rushdan

Barely escaping CIA mercenaries, ex-agent Hunter Wright is after the person who targeted his ops team, Topaz, for treason. Deputy director Kelly Russell is convinced Hunter went rogue. But now she's his only shot at getting the answers they need. Can they trust each other enough to save Topaz—and each other?

#2053 JOHN DOE COLD CASE
A Procedural Crime Story • by Amanda Stevens

The discovery of skeletal remains in a Florida cavern sends cold case detective Eve Jareau on a collision course with her past. Concealing the truth from her boss, police chief Nash Bowden, becomes impossible when the killer, hell-bent on keeping decades-old family secrets hidden, is lying in wait...to bury Eve and Nash alive.

#2054 RESOLUTE JUSTICE
by Leslie Marshman

Between hunting human traffickers and solving her father's murder, Sheriff Cassie Reed has her hands full. So finding charming PI Tyler Bishop's runaway missing niece isn't a priority—especially when he won't stop breaking the rules. But when a leak in her department brings Cassie under suspicion, joining forces with the tantalizing rebel is her only option.

SPECIAL EXCERPT FROM

◈ HARLEQUIN

INTRIGUE

When a young woman is discovered buried alive,
Colorado ME Dr. Chloe Pascale knows that the
relentless serial killer she barely escaped has found her.
To stop him, she must trust police chief
Weston Ford with her darkest secrets. But getting
too close is putting their guarded hearts at risk—and
leading into an inescapable trap...

Read on for a sneak preview of
Grave Danger,
part of the Defenders of Battle Mountain series
from Nichole Severn.

Three months ago...
When I'm done, you're going to beg me for the pain.

Chloe Pascale struggled to open her eyes. She blinked against
the brightness of the sky. Trees. Snow. Cold. Her head pounded in
rhythm to her racing heartbeat. Shuffling reached her ears as her
last memories lightninged across her mind like a half-remembered
dream. She'd gone out for a run on the trail near her house. Then...
Fear clawed at her insides, her hands curling into fists. He'd come
out of the woods. He'd... She licked her lips, her mouth dry. He'd
drugged her, but with what and how many milliliters, she wasn't
sure. The haze of unconsciousness slipped from her mind, and a
new terrifying reality forced her from ignorance. "Where am I?"

Dead leaves crunched off to her left. Her attacker's dark outline
shifted in her peripheral vision. Black ski mask. Lean build. Tall.
Well over six feet. Unfamiliar voice. Black jeans. His knees popped
as he crouched beside her, the long shovel in his left hand digging

into the soil near her head. The tip of the tool was coated in mud. Reaching a gloved hand toward her, he stroked the left side of her jawline, ear to chin, and a shiver chased down her spine against her wishes. "Don't worry, Dr. Miles. It'll all be over soon."

His voice… It sounded…off. Disguised?

"How do you know my name? What do you want?" She blinked to clear her head. The injection site at the base of her neck itched, then burned, and she brought her hands up to assess the damage. Ropes encircled her wrists, and she lifted her head from the ground. Her ankles had been bound, too. She pulled against the strands, but she couldn't break through. Then, almost as though demanding her attention, she caught sight of the refrigerator. Old. Light blue. Something out of the '50s with curves and heavy steel doors.

"I know everything about you, Chloe. Can I call you Chloe?" he asked. "I know where you live. I know where you work. I know your running route and how many hours you spend at the clinic. You really should change up your routine. Who knows who could be out there watching you? As for what I want, well, I'm going to let you figure that part out once you're inside."

Pressure built in her chest. She dug her heels into the ground, but the soil only gave way. No. No, no, no, no. This wasn't happening. Not to her. Darkness closed in around the edges of her vision, her breath coming in short bursts. Pulling at the ropes again, she locked her jaw against the scream working up her throat. She wasn't going in that refrigerator like the other victim she'd heard about on the news. Dr. Roberta Ellis. Buried alive, killed by asphyxiation. Tears burned in her eyes as he straightened and turned his back to her to finish the work he'd started with the shovel.

Don't miss
Grave Danger by Nichole Severn,
available February 2022 wherever
Harlequin books and ebooks are sold.

Harlequin.com

HIEXP0122A